I0555922

Fleet

Forgotten Worlds, Volume 5

Prudence MacLeod

Published by Prudence MacLeod, 2023.

FLEET

by
Prudence MacLeod
Copyright April 3, 2019

This is a work of fiction. Similarities to real people, places, or events are entirely coincidental.

FLEET

First edition. November 17, 2023.

ISBN: 978-1927478257

Written by Prudence MacLeod.

Cover art by Pexels

Chapter 1

Salvage

Allissandra Morgenstern sighed as she gazed at her reflection in the mirror of her small quarters. She wasn't old, but not so young anymore either. "Well, now what? You're single again, or should I say still, because it's felt like that for a long while now. So, today you finally got that promotion you've wanted for years, why aren't you happy?

"Oh, just shut up, Alli. Go to sleep and wake up happy, start the new life tomorrow." With another deep sigh, and self-admonition, she dimmed the light, softened the music, then climbed into the small bunk and closed her eyes. Sleep was a long time coming, the tears weren't.

* * * * *

The last starship, Reacher, began to slow down as she neared her destination. Both Admiral Suvi-jean Sorenson and Reacher's new captain, Captain Rhonda Moore, were on the bridge. Jeannie smiled as she listened to the voices of the bridge crew.

"We've dropped to sub-light speed, Captain."

"Shields."

"Shields are up, Captain."

"All stop."

"All stop, aye. Ship has stopped, Captain."

"Sensors, is there any sign of life anywhere in this system?"

"None so far, Captain."

"Anita, can you identify the remains of the Wrax ship?" asked Admiral Suvi-jean Sorenson.

"It's in close orbit to the first planet in the Goldilocks Zone, Admiral. No life signs on it, and no indication it has power."

"I don't trust those bastards," muttered Jeannie, as she reached for her comm unit. "Sorenson to Captain Singh."

"Here, Admiral."

"Ready your crew, you're going back to the Wrax ship to see what's what, I'll bring Fighter One and ride shotgun for you."

"Understood."

"Sorenson to SUVI 9."

"Here, Five."

"Ready F1, we're going out."

"Understood."

"Rhonda, hold your position until you hear from me. I want to make doubly certain that damn ship is dead, and there are no nasty surprises waiting for us."

"Understood, Admiral. I'll ask Anita to poke around with the sensors, see if there's anything else interesting out there while you're gone."

Suvi-jean smiled as she left the bridge, heading for the launch bay. Rhonda turned back to the big forward screen and gazed at the sea of wreckage slowly orbiting that planet. "Commander Jones, warm up the forward cannon and target that Wrax ship, you know, just in case our people need to make a fast exit."

"Aye, Captain," replied the second officer. He motioned with his hand and the gunner flipped the switch to arm the weapon.

A few moments later the man spoke. "Weapon is armed, target acquired, Commander."

"Well done, gunner. Maintain status until further orders."

"Aye, Commander, maintaining status."

"All set, Captain."

"And now we wait," said Rhonda, as she locked her gaze on the forward screen. They watched as the two small ships appeared on screen, streaking toward the derelict ship. The two ships buzzed around it for a few minutes, then one disappeared inside.

* * * * *

The ship, Retriever, settled to the partially buckled deck of the Wrax warship. "Ship has landed, Captain Singh."

"You're up, Hal. Go see if there's anything interesting on this thing."

"Aye, Captain. Kumar, anything moving on sensors?"

"Not a thing, Commander."

"Good to know. Suit up, people. We'll move in two teams; Sessas, you're with me, we'll take point. Billy, Rayla, you're with Twenty, you guys watch our backs." With that, he fastened down his helmet then led them into the airlock.

They were back in the cargo bay of the Wrax ship, but there were plenty of new damage signs, not there when they'd last entered that warship. "Retriever, there's no atmosphere, so unlikely there's anybody left alive over here. Looks like maybe a dozen of their fighter ships left we could salvage. On our way to check out the cryo room now."

"Understood. Be careful, Hal."

"Roger that," came his reply. A short while later he reported in again. "Retriever, cryo room empty, everything powered down, no life signs anywhere. Moving on."

"Understood."

A long while later he checked in again. "Retriever, much of the ship is inaccessible due to damage, the bridge is still intact, but no signs of life and no power anywhere. I'd say she's clear for salvage."

"Understood, Commander White, return to the ship. Retriever calling F1."

"Sorenson here, what's the good word, Sheila?"

"No signs of life, and no atmosphere, Admiral, maybe a dozen small fighters intact and Hal says the bridge survived. They believe she's ready for salvage if you want."

"I do want. Sheila, have your people watch over the salvage crews, just in case. I'll go home and send Olga over."

"Understood, Admiral. Retriever out." Captain Sheila Singh turned to her crew and smiled. "All right, crew, might as well relax, it'll take her a while to get things organized. We'll catch a rest while we can."

* * * * *

On the admiral's personal fighter ship, F1, Suvi-jean was smiling. "Six, take us home."

"Homeward bound, Five."

The Earalith ship, F1, moved swiftly away from the huge wreck and returned to Reacher to make a soft landing in the cargo bay. They barely touched down when Jeannie threw open the hatch and headed for the bridge, already on the comms. "Sorenson to Captain Volkov."

"Olga here, Jeannie."

"Sheila says it's ready to salvage. I'll ask Rhonda to send Moira over with you to have a look."

"Recovery One ready for flight and standing by, Admiral."

"Sorenson to Captain Moore."

"Here, Admiral."

"The wreck is ready to salvage. I'd like Moira to have a look at it, see what we can learn from it that might be useful. I've got Recovery One standing by if you're okay with this."

"I'll send her on her way, Admiral," replied Captain Moore. "Bridge to Engineering."

"Moira here, Rhonda. What's up?"

"Recovery One is standing by if you want to go over and have a look at the Wreck of the Wrax."

"On my way, Captain," came the excited reply.

"Moira, maybe take a few extra hands with you, you know, just in case you find anything useful."

"Understood and appreciated, Captain. Moira out."

"The Wreck of the Wrax?" grinned Jeannie, as she entered the bridge where Rhonda was watching the screen with Emmet and First Officer Brandon Hoffman. "Did I hear that right?"

"Sorry, Admiral, but it was too good to pass up," chuckled Rhonda. "Admiral, while you were gone I had a thought."

"Oh? Care to share?"

"We're here on a salvage mission, correct?"

"Absolutely."

"So, how about I temporarily assign Moira and some of the engineering department to you so they can oversee the main salvage operation, and you don't have to route everything through me. The main areas of Engineering could be designated to them as a salvage area under your direct command as well."

"I like it, Rhonda. Do it, and as soon as we're done here, I'll give them back."

Rhonda chuckled as she turned to Brandon. "First Officer, when the chief engineer returns, confer with her and get this set up for the admiral."

"Aye, Captain. With your permission I'll head down to Engineering and scout out the situation." She nodded, he grinned and winked at Jeannie as he walked off the bridge.

Rhonda smiled then spoke again. "Gunner, I believe we can stand down the weapon now."

"Disengaging weapon, aye. Weapon at rest, Captain."

Jeannie quirked an eyebrow at her. "Rhonda?"

"We had the Wrax ship targeted, just in case. I admit I like a bit of excitement, but I'm a cautious woman nonetheless."

Jeannie smiled brightly at her. "I knew you were the right one for the job. So, is there anything else moving out there?"

Rhonda turned to the woman on sensors. "Anita?"

"Nothing moving under its own power, Captain."

"Then we're set to go," said Jeannie, reaching for her comm. "Sorenson to Captain Drake."

"Amanda here."

"You're clear to go, Mandy. See if you can find me something good."

"Explorer Two is on the hunt," came her reply. Jeannie smiled at the excitement in her lover's voice.

"Admiral, how long do you expect us to be here?" asked Rhonda.

"Months, maybe years, Rhonda. It's hard to say. Come on, let's go to the mess and I'll give you an overview of what I hope to accomplish here."

Rhonda followed her to the mess where they each picked up a mug of the Earalithian tea and a snack. When they'd settled at the table Jeannie picked up the thread of the conversation.

"The Wrax taught us we're vulnerable, we need to up our defenses. This system is a unique gift in that there are literally dozens of ships for us to salvage.

"We can learn so much here, improve our tech, learn new designs, new types of weaponry, defensive shielding, ways to improve engine speed, ship mobility, and so much more. With luck, Amanda will find us a battleship we can repair; if not, then we'll have to build our own.

"We won't leave this system until we've picked it clean of useful information and material."

Rhonda sighed and lowered her mug to the table. "So, we're here for the long haul, now hit me with the bad news. You're going to pillage my crew, aren't you?"

Jeannie chuckled at that. "Somewhat, yes. I want you to work closely with me on this. That ship will need a full crew, and that crew will need ways to return to Reacher to spend time with friends and family."

"Jeannie?"

"Think of Reacher as the home planet. We have small ships for exploration and defense, but we need something more, a big sister to watch over Reacher. Sadly, the crew of that sister ship will not get home like the crews of the small ships do, they'll be living on the new ship.

"For example, she'll need a captain. I can't send Jake; his wives are here and not easily transferred. Carla is your chief of medical and I want her there, so Jake can't be offered the post."

"How about Hal? He'd be good."

"Lilly is attached to EX2."

"So, no Hal?"

"I won't separate families unless there is no other choice," replied Jeannie.

"What about Sheila, her new love interest could go with her."

"I like it. Sheila is a strong possibility, and Hal could captain Retriever. Yes, I like it. Okay, you've got the idea, mull it over for a while, talk to your senior staff about it and I'll do the same with the captains. There's no hurry. It could be a couple of years before we get to that stage."

"But we will get there," mused Rhonda, "so we might as well start grooming people for the new positions. For example, the new ship will need a security department. That team will have to be mined from Jake's crew. He'll need to start training people for those positions. Carla will have to start grooming people for the medical staff.

"I was right, you're going to rob me blind. How many people do you think you'll need?"

Jeannie chuckled. "Let's wait and see what we come up with for a ship." With that she rose and left the mess hall.

Rhonda stood, took the trays to the rack then leaned across the counter to thank the kitchen staff for the meal.

Chapter #2

A Work in Progress

Jake White, chief of security on the Reacher, sat gazing at his captain. Rhonda had walked in and sat down but hadn't said a word. She'd spent a couple of days mulling things over in her mind. Finally, she spoke. "Jake, promise you won't shoot me."

With a grunt of resignation, he leaned back in his chair. "You're going to rob me blind of people for Jeannie's new ship, aren't you?"

"Yes."

"Dammit, Rhonda, she's already moved most of our top people over to the small ships, now she'll want a whole crew? When?"

"Who knows, could be a couple of years, could be tomorrow if Amanda stumbles onto the right ship."

"Aw, crap." He sighed deeply then accepted the inevitable. "Okay, what do you want me to do?"

"Put some thought into who you think would be the best for the job, say ten people to begin with. Start grooming them for the positions you expect them to get. Also start grooming replacements, and you'll need at least two dozen new recruits to fill in all the holes.

"I'll send Commander Hoffman down to give you a hand organizing the whole thing. Maybe you can cherry pick a few off the small ships. Oh, and there's more. I know the admiral would love to have you as captain of the new ship, but she won't offer it because ..."

"Because I have two wives attached to this ship and she won't split us up." Jake smiled and relaxed. "I love the way a SUVI mind works. Okay, I doubt this will happen any day soon, so we've got some time. Let's do this the way Jeannie would."

Rhonda arched an eyebrow at him, and he grinned. "We look for the bright eager young people with a world of potential then promote them, right?"

She laughed at that. "You mean like she did with us? Damn fine idea, Jake. Does this mean you're going to lose another second-in-command?"

"We both know Ellen's got the experience. If she gets the job as chief of security, do you think SUVI 19 would go with her?"

"Nineteen?"

"You don't need him anymore, everybody's accepted you as captain and I, for one, can say I'm happy to have you in that role."

"Jake ..."

"I'm serious, Rhonda. Look, I've found my happy place, I have my dream job, two amazing women to love, and I'm happy right where I am. Ellen will need Nineteen, at least for the first few months. I'll be here to watch your back."

"All right, Jake, I can see the sense in that. I'll talk to Nineteen, you start the process here and we'll see how it all works out."

"He'll go," grinned Jake. "The big guy is still a security man at heart."

* * * * *

Later that day, Jake's recruitment efforts brought him to the guard room in the brig. "Hey, Marcus."

"Morning, Commander. What's up?"

Jake chuckled. "Marcus, why haven't you gone back into retirement?"

"In truth, Jake, I find I like it here. I was always content here; I like the job. I come in first thing in the morning, have coffee with the night guy, make up the crew schedule for the next week, check that the locks and doors are working properly, feed anybody we might have as a guest, then relax. I can deal with busy, you know that, but I enjoy the down times too." Marcus paused a moment before continuing.

"I had a midlife crisis, got tangled up with a wild woman, it got competitive between us, I got my ass kicked, physically and otherwise. I ended up on Recovery One, a job I didn't really want, developed issues with Sheila, then split with her, quit my job, and sulked for a while.

"I ended up back here when Rhonda was short-handed and realized this is where I belonged in the first place. I'd like to keep the job. I've got another ten or more good years in me; will you consider it?"

"Actually, I came down here to ask you to stay on a few more years," grinned Jake. "Marcus, when the admiral gets her new ship, they'll raid the hell out of us for crew and security. I'll need to train a lot of new people, and I'd really like to keep a few experienced people in key places, people I can depend on. Job's yours if you want it."

"I really do."

"Then I'm a happy man. Carry on with whatever you were doing, the brig is your baby." Jake grinned and walked away. "One down and six more to go," he mused as he turned his steps toward the mess hall. He planned to celebrate with a piece of that new cake he'd tried the day before.

* * * * *

A month passed, and all through the Reacher it was the same, on the small ships as well. Every captain understood the new ship would pull from everywhere to secure an experienced crew. The ultimate survival of the entire population could well depend on these coming choices. They had to put the best people on it.

Suvi-jean sighed as she gazed around the briefing room at her fellow SUVI. They gathered here once each week, if possible, to discuss their unique needs and/or experiences. Twenty grinned and spoke first. "So, Five, who goes and who stays?"

"What?"

"You're trying to decide which of us goes to the new ship and who stays, right?"

"We don't have a new ship yet, Twenty."

"We will," said Thirteen. "Might as well decide how to do this now so we can prepare."

"First I want your feedback on this," sighed Jeannie. "If you're not comfortable with this, I'll keep all the SUVI attached to the Reacher, keep us together."

"That would be preferred," said Three, "but it's not the best plan overall. That new ship will be somewhat more independent than the smaller ships, it will need SUVI aboard."

"Do you all agree with this?" There were several nods of agreement. "Alright then, let's decide who goes and who stays, then we meditate on that for a few days before we finalize it. Thirteen, I'll want your input before any decision is made."

Thirteen nodded so she went on. "Eighteen, your thoughts?"

"You, me, Two, Three, Thirteen, Six, Seven, Eight, Nine, Twelve, and Twenty, are all attached to the small ships which are stationed on Reacher. We must remain."

"I'll go," said Nineteen. Jeannie arched an eyebrow at him, so he grinned and went on. "Rhonda and Jake are training a chief of security for the ship. Rhonda asked me to go along as that woman's assistant. I've agreed to do so."

"Thank you, Nineteen. I have an additional task for you. The SUVI who go to that ship will need a leader, I ask that you also function in that role." He nodded his agreement, as did the others.

"I'll go," said Eleven.

"And I," agreed Fourteen.

"I'm in," smiled Sixteen.

"I'll go, they'll want help in Medical," said Four.

"Me too," said Fifteen.

"Why not, I'll go," agreed Seventeen.

"Thank you, thank you all. I admit I'm quite proud of you, and yet I'm a bit sad at having to break us up. SUVI, whenever possible we will continue to meet like this even when the new ship is in service. It's vitally important we all get to know more about each other, for we're a unique people. We need to care for and nurture each other."

"That is preferred, Admiral," smiled Eighteen. "Now, on that note, perhaps Thirteen might share his big secret with us."

Jeannie turned to Thirteen and arched an eyebrow at him. He was grinning, blushing slightly, and shaking a finger at Eighteen. "All right, all right. Connie and I have bonded and moved in together."

"You've done more than that," grinned Twenty, "right, Eighteen?"

"Right you are, Sister Twenty. You felt it too?"

"I did, should we tell him, or should we let them figure it out on their own?"

Thirteen sighed. "What are you two intuitives going on about?"

"Congratulations, you're going to be a father," grinned Twenty. "Though Eamon said it was unlikely, it was possible. Now his theory is confirmed!"

"Oh yes, not only possible, but extremely likely, I'd say," grinned Eighteen. "Brothers and sisters, we must keep this to ourselves until Connie has confirmed and made the announcement. We must not steal her moment."

"Agreed," smiled Jeannie.

"You look rather pleased with this development, Five," said Thirteen.

"I am, Thirteen. This will confirm that the SUVI can grow and thrive as well as the humans. What we are won't die with us but will continue to exist."

"The child will be born SUVI," said Eighteen. "We will all need to nurture and guide the young one as she grows."

"And so we shall," agreed Jeannie. Further discussion was interrupted by the general comms. "Engineering Salvage to Admiral Sorenson."

"Jeannie here, Moira."

"I'm back in the cargo bay, I've got some interesting toys to show you."

"Call Rhonda too, she'll want to see the treasure. I'm on my way."

Chapter #3

Found

They'd searched and pillaged the derelict ships in that system for over three months before Amanda hit pay dirt. Explorer Two's new sensors had noticed something unusual on the second planet in the Goldilocks Zone. They went down for a closer look.

"How did we manage to miss this the first time around?" asked Amanda, as they gathered in the open area for a meal while EX2 hung in low orbit over the planet.

"It must be these new sensors Engineering installed for us," said Morthel. "It was buried under a lot of dust and dirt; it would have been easy to miss. Regardless, it's there. Are we going down to take a look?"

"Yes we are, but first I want to speak to the uncertainty going around. Once the new ship comes into play, every other ship, including the Reacher will be asked to release people from their crew to man the new ship.

"So, is anybody here looking for a new job?" Only silence responded to her question. "Good to know. Now I'll share something else with you. At the last meeting of the captains, the admiral told us each captain of a small ship could designate three essential crew, everybody else could be fair game.

"The SUVI have already decided among themselves who will go and who will stay. Looks like we're stuck with Thirteen." That brought a round of chuckles.

"Three and Thirteen will stay with EX2, as will Lilly, Morthel, and Connie. Now, I hereby promote Morthel to the rank of Commander. Morthel, you're my First Officer, EX2's second in command. Do you accept the post?"

"I am honored to accept the post, Captain," smiled Morthel. A round of congratulations followed. "Does this mean I get to lead the ground missions? A captain should remain with the ship, shouldn't she?"

Amanda laughed heartily at that. "Forget it, Morthel, you're not stealing the best part of the job. Three, set us down beside that structure and we'll all go have a look."

Everyone returned to their stations, then EX2 settled to the ground beside a dome shaped structure. It had been carved from the surrounding stone and could have been easily mistaken for one. It took a lot of searching, but Morthel finally found an entrance. She called for the others, but Amanda gave her the lead, the first to enter.

Inside, the dome was small, barely big enough to fit the crew comfortably. Nothing was found except a small device atop a raised dais. Curious, they took it back to the ship and called Linsey. Linsey's ship, Friendship, arrived in short order.

The object turned out to be a recording of some kind. Morthel managed to trigger it before Captain da Silva arrived. Linsey set to work with her translation devices and soon had the message deciphered.

"Orca is a mighty ship, but the Wrax are too many. We managed to escape them by using the stealth technology, but the engines are finished. We hid the ship in a mountain pass on the eighth planet. This code will unlock the main hatch and disengage the defenses.

"It is hoped that some of our people will survive here, and with luck their descendants will be able to find and revive Orca, for that ship is the crown jewel of our accomplishments as a species. Captain Nelass, last log entry."

"Holy smokes," said Amanda.

"Shall I contact the admiral?"

"Not yet, Morthel. First we go out and have a look, see what we can see. Check your sensors, locate that eighth planet."

"Aye, Captain." A few moments later she called out. "Planet located, Captain. It's on the other side of the system from Reacher. Sending coordinates to pilot station now."

"Excellent. Linsey, do you want to tell Jeannie what I'm up to?"

"Oh heck no, I'm riding shotgun on this one. As Chief of All Things Alien, I have to check it out, don't I? Just let me get back to Friendship." She laughed with delight as she fled EX2 for her own ship.

* * * * *

The admiral was on the bridge with the captain when they heard the sudden exclamation from the sensor station. "What the heck are those two doing?"

"Anita?"

"Captain, EX2 and Friendship just took off like their tails were on fire."

"What? Comms, get me EX2."

"Aye, Admiral," came a different voice. "Reacher calling EX2, acknowledge, EX2."

"EX2 here."

"I have the admiral for you, EX2. Go ahead, Admiral."

Jeannie stepped in front of the big forward screen. "Captain Drake, where are you going in such a hurry?"

Jeannie smiled at Amanda's laugh. "Just checking out something for you, Admiral Sorenson."

"Care to share?"

"Not yet."

"Amanda, are you teasing me?"

"Yes."

"Linsey, are you listening?"

"Here, Admiral."

"Talk to me, what are you two up to?"

"Sorry, Admiral, I'm sworn to secrecy."

"You're as big a tease as Amanda. Just tell me you don't need more back up."

"We're good, Jeannie, I promise," said Amanda. "We'll confess all as soon as we're back. Please be patient with me."

"Just tell me you're not leaving the system."

"We're headed for the eighth planet."

"All right, be careful, both of you. Sorenson out." Jeannie saw the looks she was getting and sighed. "Okay, I'll admit it, that was more like a mother indulging her children than an admiral speaking to subordinate officers.

"Grandfather's trying to get me trained in proper military behavior, but apparently I'm a tough case."

"It's a work in progress?" grinned Rhonda.

"Indeed so," chuckled Jeannie. "Those two characters have found something, but they want to be sure before they spring the surprise. Anita, tell me there's nothing else moving around out there."

"Nothing but our ships, Admiral."

"Then there's no harm in letting them play. With luck they'll bring us good news. Come on, Rhonda, let's head to the mess, see if that dessert chef has any new delights for us to try."

* * * * *

EX2 swept along just above the surface of the huge planet, closing in on the coordinates supplied by the information they'd found on Planet Two. "Still nothing on sensors, Captain," said Morthel. "Wait, something, but ..."

"All stop."

"All stop, aye. Ship is stopped, Captain."

"Thank you, Three. Morthel?"

"It comes and goes, first it appears as a mountain, then as metal, then back again. There, I've got you now," she declared as she worked feverishly at the sensor adjustments. "That's a ship, Captain, no doubt, and it's huge, at least half the size of the Reacher."

"Where?"

"Right beneath us, Captain. Forty degrees hard left and a half kilometer should put us right beside it."

"Three?"

"Working, Captain."

EX2, followed closely by Friendship, turned, moved forward, then settled to the ground. Space suited figures spilled out onto the barren ground to stare at the huge ship half buried under centuries of dust. "Okay, looks like it's time for Plan B," said Amanda.

"Plan B?" asked Linsey.

"There's no way in hell we can do this on our own, Linsey."

"Yeah, you're right there. Let's start looking for the entry hatch, maybe we can find our way in before you call the admiral." She switched on the information cube from Planet Two and broadcast the entry codes. About a hundred meters away a doorway tried to open but could only manage halfway as it was partly buried in the ground.

Amanda headed for it, followed closely by the others. With a bit of work, they freed it. Linsey went in first, followed by Amanda, then the rest. The hatch closed, then the interior hatch opened, and the lights came up.

Morthel was staring intently at the instrument in her hand. Finally she nodded and unfastened her helmet. "It's a bit thin on oxygen, and pretty stale, but we can breathe it. Now that we've awakened the ship, the filters and processors will probably clean it up."

"Welcome Rylan warriors, it has been centuries since last activation," squawked the box in Linsey's hands as a voice sounded throughout the ship. "Ship is running full diagnostics."

"Ship, direct me to the bridge," said Linsey, speaking through the box. She got no response. "Okay, so not an AI, just automated responses. "All right let's try this. Weapons?"

"Weapons are offline, need repairs."

"Defensive shields?"

"Defensive shield deactivated."

With a sigh Linsey turned to Amanda. "Looks like it's all clear, want to call in the crews?"

"Yes, indeed. We did our bit, Linsey, now we let Moira and company have a go."

Amanda led the way back outside and returned to EX2. "This is EX2 calling Reacher."

"Reacher here."

"Is the admiral near?"

"Negative. One moment while I reroute. Admiral Sorenson, EX2 is calling for you."

"Go ahead."

"Jeannie, are you there?"

"Here, Mandy. You sound quite pleased with yourself."

"I am, Jeannie. We've found your ship, and she seems to be in one piece. Linsey got enough of the language to shut down her defenses, and we've had a quick poke inside. There's breathable atmosphere, but it needs work. I think it's time for Moira and Dorind to have a look at her. Sending our location to the bridge of Reacher now. EX2 out."

"Sorenson to Captain Moore."

"Rhonda here."

"EX2 found us a ship, they're sending the coordinates to you now. Get us there at all possible speed. I'll take F1 and head out."

"Understood, Admiral. We have the coordinates now, sending them on to F1." Rhonda turned to her first officer. "Commander Hoffman, recall the small ships, except for Friendship, EX2, and F1. As soon as they're aboard we'll set sail. Commander Jones, aim us at the new coordinates and prepare to move out."

"Aye, Captain. Captain, F1 is away."

"That didn't take her long," grinned Rhonda.

F1 swooped in and landed right beside EX2. Jeannie leaped out and approached. "Sorenson to EX2, permission to come aboard?"

"Granted." The hatch opened and she stepped in. A moment later there was a rush of air then the inner hatch opened, she stepped inside, removing her helmet as she walked.

"Found you a present," grinned Amanda, as she helped Jeannie out of her space suit.

Jeannie gave her a hug then stepped back to relax into a seat. "Tell me all about it."

Amanda grinned with delight as she settled down facing her. "We were going over Planet Two again when Morthel spotted something on sensors. It turned out to be a small building hidden in the rubble and dust laid down over time. We found our way in, but the only thing there was some sort of info block.

"Linsey worked her magic and decoded the message. Here, give it a listen." Jeannie sat smiling as she listened. When it finished, Amanda went on. "As you can see, we had to check it out. Linsey pulled rank as Chief of Alien Relations and came with us. The ship was right where they said it would be. We found a way in and got the defense systems shut down then called you."

"Mandy, that's amazing. Linsey is inside the ship?"

"Yeah, she's trying to convert the language to English. So, why didn't you go right there? Jeannie, sweetheart, are you going to tell me what's on your mind?"

"You are, my love, we are."

"You're going to offer me that ship, aren't you?"

"Yes. I need someone I can trust utterly aboard it. Mandy, you've proven to be our most able leader in a number of different situations. I'll be dividing my time between the two ships, so it doesn't matter which ship you're on we'll ..."

"Hush now, sweet Jeannie. You know what happens when I get a new job. Neither of us wants that; I have a much better idea. Give Sheila the ship, Hal can take over Retriever, I'll hand EX2 over to Morthel and take on that job as your personal aide."

"My sweet adorable Amanda, I love you for that, but I'm not as insecure as I was back then, and you're a lot stronger than you realize.

You're a better captain than you believe. Mandy, we will be busy, that's for certain, but we won't grow apart, neither of us will allow that."

"Jeannie, are you trying to get rid of me?"

"What??? No, Mandy no, not ever. What made you ask that?"

At that point SUVI 3 spoke up from the pilot's chair. "Admiral, may I offer you a different perspective? Forgive me, but if you want privacy, a small ship with great acoustics is the wrong place for that conversation."

Jeannie chuckled at that. "All right, Three, what did I miss?"

"Five, every captain in the fleet has a second in command, someone who can step effortlessly into the command position at a moment's notice. Every captain but you. I agree with you that Captain Drake is the most able leader under your command, therefore she should be the one to take on that role, besides, the SUVI all respect Captain Drake as a leader and would follow her."

Both Amanda and Jeannie were staring at her. Finally, Jeannie began to nod her head. "Thank you for that, Three. What you say makes perfect sense, and I have to agree with your assessment. Mandy? What do you think?"

"It makes the most sense, sweetheart. I know this spells the end of my fun days as chief explorer, but Three is right. Until recently you always had Brandon with you to look after the details, but I've noticed you fussing about that lately. Your job just got a lot bigger; you need the help."

"Yes, someone I can depend on and trust completely. You'd be perfect for that role, Mandy."

"So, we have a plan?"

"Yes, sweet Mandy, we have a plan. Three, thank you for that bit of clear-headed thinking. Sure you wouldn't like to captain the new ship?"

Three laughed at that. "Nope, sorry, the SUVI don't hold rank, just you."

"Alright then, Mandy, show me the new ship."

"With extreme pleasure," grinned Amanda, as she stepped to the transport pads. "Let's go over the easy way."

They arrived on the bridge of the new ship in a flash of light. "Linsey, tell me good things," smiled Jeannie.

"Hi, Admiral. Yes, good things, well I've got the main computer absorbing English, so that will make life a lot easier."

Just then there was a ping and a soft feminine voice spoke. "All stored information and instruction manuals successfully converted from Rylanese to English."

"There you have it, Admiral. The weapons are shut down, the shields are shut down, everything has been translated into something we can understand, but sadly, the big engines are fried. She is running on a small auxiliary power source right now."

"So, we can turn her over to Engineering?"

"Yes, but I'd like to stay around for a bit, check out the captain's log and anything else that might be of interest."

"You mean get their language into your database?"

"Yes, that," chuckled Linsey.

At that point the Reacher arrived in orbit above the new ship. "Reacher to Admiral Sorenson."

"Here, Rhonda. That didn't take you long."

"We aim to please."

Jeannie smiled at that. "All right, Rhonda. Send down Moira and team, then call the captains and your senior staff to the briefing room. It looks like it's time to have that conversation. Oh, looks like we have to go with Plan B after all."

"Roger that. Reacher out."

"Plan B?" asked Amanda.

"You were always Plan A, dear Mandy. However, I confess I do like your idea better. Let's go tuck our small ships back into the Reacher then confer with the others. It's time to start getting organized."

Chapter #4

Organizing

Jeannie and Amanda arrived at the briefing room to find everybody except Linsey waiting. "Mandy. See if you can find Morthel and Linsey for us."

Amanda nodded and smiled as she stepped out again, returning a few minutes later with Morthel and Linsey da Silva. "Everybody's here, Admiral," grinned Amanda.

"Excellent. People, EX2 has found us our new ship. A first glance tells me this ship, named the Orca by its builders, is far more than we'd dared to hope for. First, the name; it has a certain meaning in English. While it may have meant something different in the alien language, Orca is a suitable choice given their pack nature and skill at hunting together.

"Now, on to the hard decisions. Orca will need a captain and crew. Before we get to that discussion, I have two promotions to announce. Captain Drake will now be my second-in-command of the fleet and my aide. Grandfather, is there an official title for an office like that?"

"Try Vice-Admiral, that should work."

"Thank you, Captain Baris, Vice-Admiral it is. So, since that leaves EX2 without a captain, I now promote Morthel of Earalith to that post. Congratulations, Captain Morthel."

The small Earalith woman beamed her delight. "Thank you, Admiral, I swear to do all in my power to bring honor to the post."

"And I have no doubt at all that you will succeed. Now for the Orca. Whoever captains this ship will be in a unique position. Orca will be a war ship; Reacher will be the home ship. Reacher will hold our elders, children, and more, our homes. Reacher has many comforts Orca is unlikely to have. Orca's captain will need a strong, disciplined crew.

"To build this crew, the captain of the Orca will, of necessity, have to pull from Reacher for experienced people. The crews of the small ships may also lose a member or two to the Orca.

"I do expect the new captain to work with you all as she fills out her own crew."

"So, who is the new captain going to be?"

"Funny you should ask, Sheila."

"Oh come on, first you get me in trouble, won't let me retire, then you make me captain a ship, and now you want me to captain your warship? Seriously?"

"Was that a yes?" grinned Jeannie. "You can take Ernel with you."

Sheila laughed heartily at that. "All right, Jeannie, I'll do it, but I'm going to need help."

"You'll get it, Sheila. I promise. Now, let's start with your chiefs of staff. Choose those people, and then you and the captains can work from there."

"Before we get to that stage, Admiral, I'd like to wait until Moira says she's ready. Once she gives us the green light, I'd like to go over her with Brandon, decide just how much crew she'll need."

"The original ship's complement was eighteen hundred," said Linsey. "According to the captain's log, a minimum crew would be five hundred."

"Wow, okay, so let's say a thousand for a start," said Jeannie. "Once the ship is ready, and Sheila has a few weeks aboard, then we can revisit this. For the moment, Sheila, choose a minimum senior staff, then they can start working on assembling a crew."

Sheila sat nodding her head, her thoughts racing. Finally, she looked up. "Rhonda ..."

Rhonda chuckled. "You're going to rob me blind, aren't you? Okay, I've got a bridge officer for you and a chief of security. SUVI 19 has agreed to go with the security officer to help keep things running smoothly."

"Is that Ellen?"

"Yes."

"Good, I trust Ellen Brady, and she's good at her job. Who's my bridge officer?"

"Commander Jones."

"Emmet? You'd give up Emmet Jones?"

"Not willingly," said Rhonda. "Look, we have to do this like the SUVI, we have to look at the greater good. Your job will be to keep us all alive. Emmet's the best bridge officer we have, you'll need him on your ship. We talked and he's good with the transfer if you want him."

"Oh hell, you know I do. So, who do I get for a first officer?"

"Your choice," said Jeannie.

Sheila sighed and looked at Brandon Hoffman. He chuckled and shook his head. "Saw that coming. So, my soft job is over, is it?"

"She's a big ship, Brandon. You're a details man and she's a new ship. I'll need your experience until the crew can settle in and you can train a replacement."

"That'll take a few years," said Brandon. "Okay, Sheila, I'm in. Sorry, Rhonda."

"The hell you are, you're all abandoning me. I'm still a new captain and you rats are deserting the ship." She was grinning and they all smiled with her. "All right, looks like you're up, Jake."

"What? Oh no."

"Yes."

"No."

"Jake, you know I need somebody I can trust to take command if anything goes wrong, someone I can count on to keep the ship running smoothly, someone who will have my back."

Jake let his shoulders slump. "Make Hal do it. He's better at that stuff."

"Can't, the admiral will probably give him the Retriever."

She was grinning and he sighed, resigned to his fate. "All right, Captain, I'll do it. Commander Hoffman will have to give me some serious lead in time."

"I will, Jake, I'll help you all I can," said Brandon.

Sheila was smiling. "Okay, I have my first and second officers plus my chief of security. Who can I have for a chief engineer?"

"Dorind has agreed to go," said Rhonda. "He's already on the Orca with Moira, he'll have the most knowledge of the ship. He's also well respected in engineering, so the crew will accept him in that role easily enough."

"You've been working on this already, haven't you, Rhonda?"

"Admiral Sorenson and I have been at it for weeks."

"Sheila, several SUVI have volunteered to go with you as well," said Jeannie. "Nineteen will lead them; Four will go along to help in Medical."

"Speaking of Medical, Carla, I'll happily accept whoever you recommend," said Sheila.

"Harry Erdo is my second, I'll send him and let him pick his own team. If I get stuck, I'll drag poor Dr. Reilly out of his lab to help me in an emergency." Eamon grinned and winked at her.

"Who else will you need, Sheila?" asked Rhonda.

"You've got Damien Peters in Hydroponics. He was the head guy for the colony for years. I'll talk to him, see if he wants the top job again. I'll need somebody in the kitchen, and I'll need to steal somebody from Social Engagement."

"Social Engagement? Orca's a war ship, Sheila," said Jeannie.

"I know, Admiral, but there are no battles to fight right now. I know from experience how easily young eager people get bored when there's nothing going on. I'll need some ways to help them relax a bit. Give me somebody with imagination and drive. I'll need a head chef as well. Oh hell, Brandon, you decide who we need then bring them to me."

"Aye, Captain," grinned Brandon Hoffman. "Jake, as First Officer of the Reacher, you'll want to accompany me on this exercise."

"Oh yeah, that's for sure. First, I'll have to find a replacement for Chief of Security. That's not going to be easy."

"All right, friends and family," grinned Jeannie, "you've all got some serious adjustments to make, so I'll let you get to it."

* * * * *

That night Jake sighed as he entered his quarters and kicked off his boots. "What's wrong, sweetheart?" asked Carla, as she kissed his cheek and led him to the sofa. He plopped down and she sat beside him.

"Uh oh, somebody's feeling stressed," said Twenty, as she entered the room and sat at his other side.

"Yeah, the hammer fell today."

"What? I had that ..."

"No honey, not your war hammer. What I mean is, they found the new ship today, Sheila Singh is the new captain for it, and she raided the hell out of us."

As her joke fell flat, Twenty leaned into him supportively, "Yes, but you were expecting that. You were prepared, right?"

"Wasn't prepared for this," he sighed.

"Oh dear, I think our boy got promoted," said Twenty.

"Right on the money. Sheila snagged Reacher's first and second officers as well as the one we trained to lead security for them."

"Brandon and Emmet Jones both?"

"Yup. Both of them."

"And you got Brandon's job, right?"

"Yes, Twenty, I'm the new first officer on the Reacher."

"I sense Jeannie's gentle hand behind this one."

"Twenty?"

"Think about it, guys. If anything happens to Rhonda, she'll need someone she knows and trusts to step in and take over."

"Yeah, that makes sense," said Carla. "Jake, you can handle the job, what's the big problem? I saw how reluctant you were in the meeting, what's the issue?"

"She left me empty for Security. I had that one under control, but she pulled me out and now Security is wide open. I've got nobody I feel comfortable putting in that office. I am so screwed."

"Ask Hal."

"Twenty, he really wants to be the captain of Retriever."

"Between you and me, I think he'd be open to the idea. Hal knows security, he always aspired to the top job. I think he decided to go with hunting the captain's job because he couldn't see any way past you to get to the top of security. Talk to him, lover, see what he says."

"Do you really think he'd be open to the idea?"

"When was the last time she was wrong about stuff like that?" grinned Carla.

"Good point. All right, girls, I'll talk to Hal in the morning, but I'll call in reinforcements."

"Reinforcements?"

"Yes, my lady loves, reinforcements; Jeannie, Mandy, and Rhonda."

* * * * *

Next morning Hal answered the summons from Jeannie to meet him in the briefing room of the Reacher. That alone told him something was up. He'd heard the night before that Sheila had been given command of the new warship, could this mean he was getting his promotion to captain sooner than expected? He was hopeful.

As soon as he stepped through the door he knew something big was up. Jeannie was there with Amanda, Jake, and Rhonda. Hesitantly, he approached the table. "Reporting as requested, Admiral."

"Relax, Hal, have a seat," said Jeannie.

He sat, watching Jeannie carefully. "Suvi-jean, what are you up to now?"

"She's done it again, Hal. Your dream is about to come true," grinned Jake. "Now we see if you're able to handle it."

Hal looked from his brother to Jeannie then back again. "Okay, I can see the world's gone all to hell again. Lay it out for me."

Jake leaned his elbows on the table and sighed. "Hal, Captain Singh has been given the Orca, the new warship. I'm sure you knew that already. What you might not know is she's robbing us blind for crew. Both Brandon Hoffman and Emmet Jones went with her.

"Rhonda then promoted me to First Officer of the Reacher. That left a big hole in Security. Commander Hoffman is gone, Sheila Singh is gone, as is Ellen Brady who went to the Orca as well, and of course, Rhonda."

"That's where you come in, Hal," said Rhonda. "We need you as Chief of Security. I know you wanted to captain a small ship, but as Security Chief you'll have EX4 at your disposal, so you get both dreams, the top job in Security and a small ship."

Hal drew a deep breath and slowly released it. "Wow, Jeannie, you did it again. I guess I now have to forgive you for beating me up when you first came aboard the Reacher."

"Does that mean you'll do it?" asked Jeannie, a merry twinkle in her eye.

"Absolutely, if you guys are serious."

"We are," replied Rhonda. "Congratulations, Chief of Security. All right, Admiral, he's all yours. Jake, let's go, we've got a lot of work to do."

With that they rose and left, leaving Hal with Jeannie and Amanda. He looked from one to the other. "Guys?"

"Hal, Retriever has been gutted by these promotions," said Amanda. "In recent weeks she's lost her captain, first officer, and two of her most effective infiltrators. We'd like your advice on what we should do here."

Hal took a deep breath then slowly released it. "You won't like it."

"Hal?"

"By far the best leader on Retriever right now is a woman I'd follow anywhere, anytime, if she were captain, but there are issues."

"Talk to me, Hal," said Jeannie.

"It's Sessas, Jeannie. Girl has a keen mind and can make decisions, quality decisions, under fire. Her main motivation is like a SUVI, protect the clan, as she calls it. The problem is communication. She's not a big talker."

"Hal, are you serious? You are, you're serious."

"I am. I'd say Twenty, but she's SUVI and won't take it. Sessas is the next best bet, in fact she often flings orders and Twenty follows them instantly and without question anyway."

"Would the crew follow her?"

"I believe so; Twenty would skin 'em alive if they didn't. Sessas likes Kumar, they joke a lot together. He'd be a good first officer for her, Billy or Rayla could lead the infiltrators."

"My god, Hal, you truly are serious. All right, Mandy, call her here and we'll talk to her about it. Call Twenty as well, I'll want her take on it."

Amanda grinned as she reached for her comm. "Sessas and SUVI 20 to the bridge briefing room. Repeat, Sessas and SUVI 20 to the briefing room."

"On our way," responded Twenty. They arrived moments later. "What's up?"

Jeannie smiled as she leaned her elbows on the table. "Sit down, relax. When we called, you responded, Twenty, what were you two doing?"

"We were on the Retriever; Sessas was making us do inventory."

Jeannie chuckled at that. "Inventory, Sessas?"

"Captain gone, First Officer not there. Nobody working ship. Ship must be ready if needed. Take inventory, top up supplies, weapons, medical."

Jeannie was nodding her head. "Twenty, my beloved sister, I need a favor."

"Name it and it's yours, Jeannie, you know that. Anything at all. Tell me, what do you need?"

"You and Sessas make a good team, don't you?"

"We're a great team, right Sister Sessas?"

Sessas nodded, never taking her eyes off Jeannie. "Yes, good team. Sessas think Admiral Jeannie up to something."

Jeannie laughed then gave Sessas her full attention. "Sessas, do you fully understand what the captain of a ship does? What she must do?"

"Captain leader, like chief of clan, make decisions, give direction, guide people, protect, nurture."

"Do you understand the task of the Retriever ship?"

"Retriever search, rescue, keep safe, bring home."

Jeannie nodded. "Sessas, I have seriously underestimated you, and I apologize for that. Sessas, I need a new captain for the Retriever. Will you be that captain for me?"

"Sessas be captain?"

"Yes. Hal believes you would be a good captain, and I'm starting to agree with him. Will you do this for me?"

"Sessas do, help SUVI 5 protect people, clan. Sessas do best she can."

"Then I promote you to the rank of captain. Captain Sessas, the Retriever is yours." Sessas squeaked with delight.

"Jeannie, what was the favor you wanted? Do you need me to stay with Sessas to watch her back?"

"In a word, Twenty, yes. You two make a good team and she'll need your support."

"She'll have it. Sister Sessas and I are a package deal, right Sessas?"

"Tentee good sister, we good team. We make good captain, yes?"

"Yes, I'll help you make a good captain. Jeannie, between us, I think you made the right decision here. Sessas is practically running the ship now anyway. She deserves to be recognized for her contribution."

"I'll expect you to accompany her to all captains' meetings as well."

"Understood."

"Alright then, Sessas, go get a captain's coat on, then we'll go back to Retriever and announce your new position. Hal has been promoted to Chief of Security for Reacher, so you'll need to fill out your crew."

"Sessas understand." An hour later a Saurian woman who communicated mostly through the language box attached to her uniform, was seated in the captain's chair of Retriever. It was hard to tell, but it looked like she was smiling. SUVI 20 had a huge grin on her face as she watched her friend.

"Kumar."

"Yes, Captain Sessas?"

"You First Officer, rank commander. Billee."

"Captain?"

"You commander now, lead Strikers. Need people. Go talk to Hal, find new Strikers."

"Aye, Captain. I'm on it." Twenty winked at him as he left the ship. This was going to work; the crew would respond to Sessas.

* * * * *

While Sessas was being introduced to the Retriever as the new captain, Rhonda walked on the bridge of the Reacher. "Sub-Commander Anita Ortega."

Anita looked up from her sensors with wide eyes. "Captain Moore?"

"Commander Jones has abandoned us for the Orca. I now promote you to the rank of commander. I need a Second Officer, someone to run the bridge, will you accept the position?"

"I will, Captain, thank you. I'll do my best to bring honor to the post."

Rhonda grinned at her. "You'll need to train a back-up too."

"Yes, Captain. Did I get the rumor right, Commander Hoffman took a transfer too?"

"He did. I promoted Jake White to First Officer, then he recruited his brother Hal to take over at Security. I think we'll come out of this in good shape, Anita."

"Good to know, Captain."

"All right, I'll leave you to it." With that, Rhonda turned and walked off the bridge. Anita made eye contact with an Earalithian man and pointed to the sensor panel. With an eager smile, he hurried over.

Chapter #5

Scrambling

The next day Jeannie, Amanda, and Sheila found Moira Duncan in the Engineering section of the Orca. She was studying a schematic on the screen before her. Moira started to rise, but Jeannie waved her back. "Moira, tell me good things."

Moira chuckled at that. "I've got tons of good news for you, Jeannie. First, this ship is amazing, and we're learning lots of things that will be useful overall. Just as the Wrax were a warrior race, the Rylan were peaceful explorers.

"However, they soon learned that sometimes peace has to be defended, and the people protected from aggressors. In response to that, they built this ship. She carried a hundred small fighters, but they're all gone, probably lost in the battle with the Wrax. Orca also has these amazing shields, which I'm hoping I can duplicate and install on all our ships."

"Tell me about them, Moira."

"Jeannie, they're stronger than ours, and they scatter any sensor's attempt to target them. Morthel had to reconfigure her sensors three times to pick up the ship. The shield doesn't make you invisible, but damn close to it, and nearly impossible to target effectively. Big bonus for Rhonda, it's possible to shoot through them. Now I just have to figure out how they did it.

"Besides that, their metals are close to Earalithian, so I believe we can fix or duplicate whatever we might need for repairs."

"That's wonderful, Moira, now tell me the bad news."

"Bad news?"

"I can feel it from you, Moira. What don't you want to tell me?"

"We need more trained engineers, and we don't have them. We're trying to train new people, pulling from all departments as well as the passengers, but the problem is we're still learning as we go ourselves.

43

It'll take months just to figure out everything this ship can do, what's needed for daily running, etc."

Sheila sighed. "How many months, Moira?"

"Couple of years' worth at least," was the soft reply.

"Seriously?"

"Sheila, this ship is highly weaponized. You could come over here too soon and an untried officer flip a switch thinking it does one thing, but instead it blows Reacher out of the sky. Dorind and I will need a year to figure out what everything does, then you'll need another year to familiarize a crew."

"Then we'll use those years to start training those crews," said Jeannie. "Will she fly now?"

"What??? Probably, but ... Jeannie, what are you thinking? We won't dare take this ship interstellar even if we can repair the engines."

"Not interstellar, interplanetary."

"Jeannie?"

"Moira, you're working against heavier gravity that you like, on a planet with no atmosphere. Planet Two, where Mandy found the remains of the Rylan attempt to colonize, has a breathable atmosphere, and lighter gravity. It'll be easier to work there, and different crews can train there in the open, plus you'll be a lot closer to the other derelicts for scrap metal.

"More, you say Dorind can help us set up a smelter operation, make the metals you need. Wouldn't a planet be a better site for that than a ship? You'll also want to top up the Reacher's supplies before we leave this system, and I expect Dorind will want to do the same for Orca.

"So I ask again, does she have enough power to get her to Planet Two?"

Moira sighed and thought for a moment. "No, she doesn't, not right now. Jeannie, what you say makes perfect sense. The gravity here is too strong for the auxiliary power to get us into space. If we could reach orbit, then we could make it. After all, that's how she got here in the first place."

"Could the small ships add enough lift to get you up to orbit?"

Moira chuckled. "Yes, probably. We'll have to grapple them all onto Orca, then it could work. Want to try it?"

"I do. Talk it over with Dorind, if the two of you agree, then make it happen. Sheila, get your bridge crew over here and start learning what you'll need to do to get her to Planet Two."

"On it, Admiral," grinned Sheila.

Jeannie turned to Amanda as Sheila walked away.

"Meeting with the captains?"

"Yes, Mandy, my bewitchingly beautiful companion, a meeting with the captains first thing tomorrow."

"Call in Miriam as well?"

"Yes love, the passenger representatives as well. I expect we'll have to draw more heavily on them in the coming days. Moira, I'll want you there, too."

"All right, Jeannie. I'll see if I can have some answers for you by then."

"Then we'll let you work," smiled Jeannie, as she took Amanda's hand and called for transport back to Reacher. They disappeared deom the Orca to reappear aboard the Reacher.

* * * * *

It was early the next morning; Amanda stifled a yawn as she spoke. "Everybody's here, Admiral Sorenson."

"Thank you, Vice-Admiral Drake," grinned Jeannie as she winked at Amanda. "Moira, what's the good word, will it work? Can we bring Orca into a better work area?"

"Yes, Admiral, it should work. It'll take a few days to get all the small ships hooked on, and then we can give it a go."

"Sheila, tell me you can fly her without shooting the rest of us out of the sky."

"Yes, we can. We won't take a gunner with us and there'll be no one at the weapons station."

"All right then, we're good to go. Time to bring you all into the loop. We're going to lift Orca off this planet and take her back to Planet Two where it'll be easier to work on her.

"Also, on Planet Two we're planning to set up a smelting operation where we can create metals for our ships. There'll be a demand for workers, ship crews to be trained, and more. Spread the word, anybody who wants to work will be welcomed. I'm told it'll be two years or more before we've completed our salvage operation in this system.

"Now, here's what we'll need from you captains. Rhonda, your ship is the home ship. With everybody working we'll need everything you've got for medical, food service, and social engagement up and running.

"Olga, your two ships will be assigned to Moira for engineering needs. Morthel, Sessas, you two will fly regular patrols, making sure we're still alone in this system. Reacher will be scanning as well, but I want you two patrolling." Both Sessas and Morthel nodded that they understood.

"EX4 will remain behind or not, as needed, under the command of Reacher's Chief of Security. Linsey, stay close to Reacher, but make yourself available to Moira as required."

"Aye, Admiral."

"Once we have Orca settled in her new home, work will resume on getting her functional and manned with a full crew. Now, while Moira's working on the ship, Sheila will be gathering her crew and seeing to their training. Linsey, you may have to help with translating instruction manuals and such.

"Sessas, have you managed to rebuild a crew for Retriever?"

"Have full crew, need training time. Patrolling is good, can train on job."

Jeannie smiled at that. "Morthel, do you have a full crew?"

"I do, Admiral. Thirteen has been doing some recruiting. Admiral, since we won't be doing a lot of exploring for the near future, do you want me to assign some of my maintenance men to Engineering for the Orca?"

"I could sure use them, Morthel," said Moira.

"Then, with the Admiral's permission, I'll send four of the six over."

"Permission granted, Morthel. People, everything we can do to help each other will speed up the process.

"It's not that we're in a hurry to leave this system, the hurry is to get Orca up to full power and get the rest of our ships fully manned and ready as well. The next time we set sail I want us to be fully confident in our ability to defend ourselves if we have to.

"We got lucky in that last battle, Brandon managed to thin out the enemy for us, but if the Wrax had caught us by surprise, we'd have been wiped out. We learned a strong lesson there, and we need to heed that warning."

* * * * *

While that meeting was going on, Hal White had a visitor in his office. "Come in, come in and shut the door." The young woman entered closing the door behind her. "Take a seat. Now, who are you and what do you want?"

"Sir?"

Hal sighed and relaxed back in his chair. "Sorry. I got dropped into this job a few days ago, no second-in-command to help me, the guy who works the office is off with a broken thumb from training, and I have no idea at all what the hell is going on.

"So, I'm Commander Hal White, Chief of Security, and you are?"

"Ebony Graves, sir."

"How can I be of service, Ms. Graves?"

"I'm wondering about my status, sir."

"Your status?"

"Yes, sir. My grandfather is the pilot of EX4. He worked a deal with Commander White, your brother, to get me into that position."

"A deal, huh. What was the deal?"

"I had to pass the security training, then Grandfather would train me for his job."

"And Jake went for it?"

"Yes, sir, but then it got crazy, and Commander Moore was in charge. I talked to her, and she was okay with it, then ..."

"First Rhonda, then Jake got promoted and now I'm here. So tell me, how is it going with the training?"

"I passed, got my badge this morning. The instructor said I was the fastest one through the training he could remember, except for you and your brother."

"Yeah, we grew up on that training, it was second nature."

"I did the same with fighter pilot."

"VR games?"

"Yep, ever since I was ten. I hold the record on the ship for highest level achieved."

"I thought I held that record."

"Until last week," she grinned.

"Okay, hot shot, so you want to know if I'll keep the bargain." He grinned and went on. "I will, but here's the deal. I put you on that front desk and you don't let anybody in unless you believe there's no option."

"Sir?"

"You passed the training, this is your first security post, Officer Graves, deal with it. Look, girl, things are nuts right now. Give me a chance to settle in, then I'll send you out with EX4 so you can train. I'll stick to the bargain, but you have to help me out in the meantime. Okay?"

"Deal. Sir, I can't thank you enough for this."

"Get me a few minutes peace to catch my breath, and I'll call it even. Go on now, get out there and get to work." He was still grinning as she fled the office.

A few minutes later he heard her voice. "I'm sorry Ensign, but Commander White is extremely busy. I'll put your name on the list, and he'll contact you as soon as he can. I'm sorry, but it's the best I can do."

Hal nodded his approval then returned to the list of officers before him. Somebody was going to unexpectedly find themselves promoted to second-in-command of security on the Reacher. An hour later he contacted Rhonda and Jake, asking for a conference.

They met in his office. Hal told them who he wanted to promote to second-in-command. Jake sighed. "Damn, Hal, are you sure about this?"

"I can't grab Billy or Sessas will have my hide and you know it. Truth is, I want Rayla on the Retriever too. Retriever needs the best strikers available, so, of the people who're left, Kar's my best bet. She was with me against the grounders and didn't melt under fire."

"Yes, but she's got seven excessive force marks on her record."

"I know, she'll have to tame it down a bit. Rhonda, what do you think?"

"I think she'll do fine. Most of those reprimands are a result of complaints from an ex-boyfriend who wouldn't take piss off for an answer. Every time he'd grab her, she'd flatten him, and then he'd go whining to Commander Hoffman. Hoffman gave her the reprimands but refused to bust her down. I think he secretly wanted to promote her.

"You'll have to work closely with her, but I think she'll do, provided Sheila hasn't already recruited her."

"Damn that woman, she's picked us clean already," sighed Jake.

Rhonda chuckled at that. "Yes, but think about it, Jake. The three of us got promoted higher than we ever expected to go this fast, and we've all proven ourselves. Now we have to offer the same opportunity for others to shine and help them do it. Call her in, Hal, promote her, and hold on to your hat."

"Thanks, I think. Okay, Kar it is, thanks guys."

"Good luck," chuckled Rhonda, as she and Jake left.

"Thanks, I'll need it." Hal reached for his inter office comm. "Ebony, call Ensign Karissa Glenn to my office then come in with her and shut the door behind you." With wide eyes, Ebony reached for the ship wide comm.

* * * * *

In the kitchens, Allisandra sighed as she gazed out at the people in the mess. She saw a woman she'd once had a crush on years before. It was the woman's smile that had first attracted her, but in recent years the girl hadn't smiled a lot. Worse, she had no idea Alli even existed.

Alli pushed down hard on her shy nature and decided to talk to the woman, see if she could put a smile back on that exquisite face. She was barely halfway to the woman's table when the object of her desire got a call on the comms and rose to stride swiftly away. Alli sighed and went back to work.

* * * * *

Hal was sitting at his desk, reading from the screen as the two women entered and closed the door. "Ensign Glenn reporting as requested, Commander."

"Mmm, Ensign Glenn, I see by your record that you have seven reprimands for excessive force. Commander Hoffman has eight, the most of any officer on this ship. Are you going for the record?"

The tall woman swallowed hard before she replied. "No, Commander."

"Good, because that would be a poor ambition for the second-in-command of Security." Hal looked up and chuckled at the wide-eyed woman standing so stiffly at his desk. "Sit down and relax, both of you. You heard me right, Sub-Commander Glenn, the job's yours if you want it."

Kar's mouth worked a few times before she managed to make a sound. She'd been expecting another reprimand. "Yes, oh my god, yes, I want it. Thank you, I'll do everything I can to bring honor to the post."

"I'll help you all I can, Kar. Look, I'm new here too. We'll work together and watch each other's backs. Kar, we're in the soup here, Captain Singh has robbed us blind and we're up to our collective asses in new recruits. We've got to make a solid security force out of them. Are you with me?"

"Yes sir, I'm with you all the way."

"You were expecting another complaint, weren't you?"

"Yeah, I was."

"It's here on file, lodged yesterday."

"Sir, I ..."

"Guy won't take no for an answer?"

"Every time he comes at me I try to walk away, but he grabs me."

"And then you deck him?"

She allowed her shoulders to sag. "Yes."

"We'll deal with that in a minute. First, let me introduce you to my new aide, Ensign Ebony Graves. Ensign Graves, this woman is Sub-Commander Glenn, my second-in-command."

It was Ebony's turn to stare at him wide eyed. "Sir, did you just promote me?"

"Ebony, for a woman who spent the last ten years in VR trying to break my record at fighter pilot, you have somehow managed to acquire mad people skills. Jeannie Sorenson was on this ship one day when she made Ensign and became the Captain's eyes and ears. You missed that record by three days.

"Ebony, you're good at your job, I want to keep you there on the front desk, but I did make you a promise. So, here's the deal, you're my aide, but also the pilot of EX4. When that ship goes out, you'll be at the helm.

"Now, go back to your desk and send two officers to arrest this man." He spun the screen around for them, Kar's ex-boyfriend was on the screen.

"As soon as they're on the way, get to EX4 and start your pilot training. Don't come back to me until you feel confident you can fly her, then we'll all go for your first flight."

With a wide grin of pure delight, she leapt to her feet and fled his office. They soon heard her outside, assigning two officers to the task.

"Sir ..."

"Hal. Kar, we've worked together a lot in the past, and here we are again. Hal's fine in private."

"Thanks, Hal. Can you tell me why you're arresting Frell?"

"That man's messing you up, trying to destroy your career, almost succeeded. It was Rhonda who clued me in to what was going on. I'll toss him in the brig for a few days then offer him a six month stay or he can volunteer for the Orca. That should put a stop to this crap. Oh, I'm not going to process this latest complaint, so you don't tie the record."

She smiled at last. "Thanks for that. Hal, why me? I heard about Jake getting promoted and was relieved when you took this position, I just didn't expect to become your second. I was sure Billy or Rayla would be it."

"Kar, I told Jake and Rhonda that Sessas would skin me if I raided her crew, but strictly between us, I was looking for a way to give you the job."

"Seriously? Why?"

"Because you have the potential, but you've been getting a raw deal. I've had my nose in these records and reports for days now. Every time you start to shine there's a complaint and you pull back. Kar, I know what it's like to have circumstances hijack your ambitions. Jake beat me to this job, then it looked like Rhonda would be next, and then Ellen.

"I got lucky, and now so have you. I know you can do this. Go get a new uniform and then come back ready to work, we've got a ton to do."

"Back in a flash," she grinned as she fled the office. On her way back to her quarters she saw her ex being hauled off to the brig. Finally, someone had seen through his manipulative nature. She'd been given her chance and meant to seize it.

As she changed into a fresh uniform and pinned her shiny new Sub-Commander insignia to it, she spoke to the woman in the mirror. "He knew. He knew and understood, and he's making it stop. I finally get a chance to show what I can do. I will not let this man down."

* * * * *

Hal walked into the brig area and nodded to the man stationed there. "Marcus, Jake says you're willing to stay on."

"I am, Commander. I like it here."

"I'm relieved to hear it. Now, I need a favor."

"Name it."

"I need you to shut down all the recording devices for a few minutes."

Marcus grinned as he worked. "Recording devices shutting down for regular diagnostics in three, two, one; recording devices are offline, back up in five minutes. Do what you need to do, Commander and I'll log this, could take me awhile."

The man in the cell was looking nervous. "What the hell's going on here?"

"I'm here to explain the facts of life to you," replied Hal, as he stepped closer to the cell. "I'll use small words so you can understand. You've been trying to sabotage an officer's career. Today you were arrested for making excessive unfounded complaints, complaints I don't have the staff or desire to deal with. If you want out of here to stay, listen close.

"Mess with me and I'll have you charged with deliberately trying to interfere with the smooth operation of Reacher's security. Trust me, the captain will take a dim view of that one. You'll be looking at two years or more in here."

"That's pure bullshit. I demand a trial; I'm entitled to a trial."

"Yes, you are. If you elect the trial you'll face my brother as judge, me as the prosecutor, and my second officer as your defender. Her name is Sub-Commander Karissa Glenn, maybe you know her. If that's the way you want to go, I can arrange it.

"However, there's another way, a way that lets you out of here free and clear."

"Okay, how does that work?"

"I let you out, you haul your sad sorry ass down to Commander Hoffman's office and beg for a job on the Orca, then you move your quarters over to the area designated for Orca's crew. You avoid Sub-Commander Glenn like the plague, and never give me cause to regret what I've done here. Is it a deal?"

Beaten, the man hung his head. "Deal. She'll never see my face again."

"Recording devices back on line in three, two, one. We're up and running, Commander White."

"Thank you, Marcus. You can let him go now; he has an appointment with Commander Hoffman." Marcus grinned as Hal walked out. He flipped the switch and the cell door slid open.

* * * * *

A few hours later, as Kar sat in the mess enjoying her dinner, she was smiling. Unfortunately, Alli was too busy to notice.

Chapter #6

New to the Job

Two more months passed with the captains trying to organize and reorganize their crews. Some days it went smooth, others not so much. "What the ...? Commander, EX4 just launched, looks like someone has stolen it."

"Explain," said Anita, as she stepped closer to the man on sensors.

"It's flying wild, erratic, almost out of control. EX2 and Retriever are in pursuit."

"Weapons, lock new laser guns on EX4, disable their engines on my mark. Comms, get me EX4."

"Aye, Commander. Reacher calling EX4, Reacher to EX4, respond or be fired upon."

"EX4 here, I'm a bit busy right now," came Hal's voice.

"Doing what, exactly?" asked Anita, as she stepped in front of the screen.

"Flying maneuvers and trying to keep my breakfast where it belongs and not in my lap. Don't you dare fire on my ship. EX4 out."

"Dammit, he cut me off. Stand down weapons. Bridge to Captain Moore."

"Right behind you, Anita," chuckled Rhonda, as she stepped onto the bridge. "I was on my way here to let you know EX4 would be flying maneuvers with EX2 and Retriever this morning. Jake stopped me to discuss an issue, so I didn't get here in time."

She stepped to sensors for a look. "Well now, looks like Hal's new pilot's a real hot shot. Did he say how she's doing?"

Anita grinned as she replied. "He said he was trying to keep his breakfast down. When did he come up with this idea?"

"He didn't, it was Captain Morthel. She and Captain Sessas have been flying patrols and started doing this on their own. The admiral liked it, so she put EX4 into the mix, then Hal put his new aide in the pilot's chair. Gotta give her credit, the girl can sure fly."

"That she can," agreed Anita. "I need to have a talk with the chief of security when he gets back, though."

"Oh?"

"The bridge needs to know about things like this before they happen, so we don't fire on the fleeing ship."

"You're right, Anita, but this one's on me. Hal informed me before he left."

"Wrong choice."

"Excuse me?"

"He should have informed the bridge first, this is where everything flows from, this is where the sensors and weapons controls are, this ..."

"Point taken. You're absolutely right; I'll deal with this right now." Rhonda reached for her comm. "Captain to First Officer White."

"White here."

"Jake, I want a full meeting of all senior staff first thing tomorrow, everybody there, no exceptions. If they're breathing, I want them there."

"Aye, Captain. Shall I inform the passenger reps as well?"

"No, this is strictly ship's crew business."

"Aye, Captain, full senior staff meeting, 0:800 tomorrow. I'll inform the senior staff."

* * * * *

Next morning they filed in while Rhonda paced. "All senior staff present, Captain Moore."

"Thank you, Commander White. People, we came close to making a terrible mistake yesterday, a rookie mistake. Therein lies the problem, too many of us are rookies in these jobs, and we need to sharpen up.

"Yesterday I was informed EX4 would be flying maneuvers with EX2 and Retriever. I was on my way to the bridge to let Anita know what was going on, but Jake stopped me for a couple of minutes. In the few minutes we discussed another matter, Hal launched EX4.

"No big deal, really, but here's where it almost went dangerously sideways. We have new weapons on this ship, small arms compared to the main cannon, but more than adequate to knock down EX4.

"EX4 was flying erratically, fleeing from EX2 and Retriever. The bridge, believing EX4 might have been stolen, targeted the ship then called them on comms. If Hal had delayed any longer to respond, Anita would have fired attempting to disable the fleeing ship.

"People, we screwed up big time here, we've gotten complacent just sitting here in orbit watching everybody else do the work. We were slack and nearly paid for it. That's not going to happen again.

"Engineering, the launch bay is in your department. From now on, no ship launches, and no ship lands without the bridge being informed first and giving clearance."

"Understood, Captain," replied the older man who was the acting Chief Engineer. "I'll inform launch bay immediately, then overhaul the procedures to accommodate the new standing orders."

Rhonda nodded, then sank back into her chair. "Okay, that was the big one, but every department needs to sharpen up. We need to talk to each other, people, we need to keep everybody in the loop, especially when it concerns the operation of this ship.

"Yesterday's near disaster pointed out to me just how vulnerable we are right now. We're the new kids here, and we're not working together as a team, we're all running around on our own trying to figure things out as we go. That won't work; we need to help each other.

"Yesterday, I stepped onto the bridge and into an emergency situation. I swiftly discovered my own oversight, not informing the bridge immediately of the maneuvers, nearly caused a disaster. I was then gently rebuked by the second officer, and had it made clear to me that the bridge is the beating heart and thinking brain of the ship. They need to know what's going on before it happens.

"Anita, I'll admit your tone yesterday rubbed my fur the wrong way a bit, but you were right to speak. However, as a favor to your captain, next time you chew me out, could you do it in private? It's embarrassing for the captain to be chastised in front of the crew."

Cheeks red with embarrassment, Anita studied her hands. "Aye, Captain. I apologize, you're right, I should have asked to speak in private."

"Accepted, but you were right to speak. Anita, the way that incident unfolded yesterday told me the only department on this ship functioning at peak efficiency is the bridge. You handled the situation perfectly and professionally."

"Except the part where I barked at you?" grinned Anita.

"Yeah, that," replied Rhonda, matching her grin. "People, don't be afraid to speak to me if you feel strongly about something, just keep it professional. I promise to do the same for you.

"Now, let's start working together as a team, because that's what we're supposed to be. Reacher is the mother ship, the home of humanity, the last refuge of our species and those we've gathered to us. They depend on Reacher for survival, and Reacher depends on us to function. We need to sharpen up.

"On that note, Hal, report."

"Aye, Captain. I'm slowly getting settled into the job. I've promoted Karissa Glenn to my second-in-command and given her the rank of Sub-Commander. I was then less than subtly informed by the first officer that the promotion should have come from you.

"I appointed a new graduate to be my aide and to pilot the EX4. She's a heck of a pilot, and even better as an aide. Jake reinstated Marcus full time at the brig, and I backed that up. We've got all the empty slots in the roster filled with recruits, but they're raw. We're teaming them up with the older, more experienced, officers until they prove up.

"Otherwise, all's quiet."

"Then I'm happy. Engineering?"

"We're still shorthanded, Captain, but managing. We're training new people as fast as we can, but a good engineer isn't made overnight, and engineering is advancing every day. However, we're managing; Reacher is solid and fully functional. There are no outstanding issues."

"Bridge?"

Anita smiled. "We had new weapons installed last week and almost had a chance to give them a field test. The new sensors reach further out and respond faster. All in all, the bridge is in good shape and I'm happy with the crew's response times in an emergency situation."

"Then it looks like we're good. People, I need you to work together, and believe me when I say, if in doubt at all, come to me. Know that I'll do all I can to help you, but I need the same in return. Meeting adjourned."

"Captain, a word in private?"

"Chief of Medical, you're not going to chew me out, are you?" grinned Rhonda.

"No, ma,am," came the laughing reply. "It's a different issue, but not for the general staff."

"Understood. Off to work, people." She waited until the others had left the room. "What's up, Carla?"

"You are, Rhonda. First, let me say you're doing a hell of a job as captain. We were all shocked that Jeannie let go of the reigns, then surprised that she raised you up. I'm delighted to say we're all relieved that you're up to the task; it's like still having Jeannie at the helm, you think a lot alike."

"That's high praise indeed, Carla, and I thank you for it. Tell me, did I sense a *but* in there somewhere?"

"No buts, Captain, more of an *I feel your pain*. Rhonda, I know what you're dealing with here. I was just another medic until Jeannie arrived and turned everything upside down. Suddenly I was Chief Medical Officer; me, barely thirty years old, scared to death of screwing it up or worse.

"My point is, I understand some of what you're facing every day, and if you want to just hang out and have a good rant, meltdown, or general bitch session, my office is a safe haven, and you'll always find a sympathetic ear there."

"Thank you for that, Carla. I'll admit, the idea of a meltdown has had appeal a few times, and my poor mirror has listened to a rant or two. I promise I'll take you up on the offer once in a while."

Carla smiled as she rose to go. "Any time at all, Captain. Any time at all."

As Rhonda rose to leave the room, she heard Hal outside talking to Anita. Rhonda knew Hal well and grinned as she listened.

"Commander Ortega, a word please?"

"Commander White?"

"You targeted my ship?"

"EX4 was flying erratic, EX2 and Retriever in pursuit, the ship appeared to have been stolen. The idea was to disable the engines if we got no response."

Anita began to relax as she saw the grin spread across his face. "Good job, Anita; I'd have done the same thing. It's good to know that, with the rest of us stumbling around in the dark, the bridge is still in top form. Well done."

She just rolled her eyes and shook her head as he walked away. Working with the two crazy White brothers was going to be interesting, to say the least.

* * * * *

Hal was nearing the Security lunchroom when voices stopped him cold. "I don't know, Jim, but it's all gone to hell lately. Shit, that SUVI promoted the lizard to captain of the Retriever. I pulled my app for a post there in a hurry, I can tell you."

A grunt was the only response he got, so the fool kept talking. "Yeah, and now Karissa is second in command. I can only imagine what she did for Hal to get that job."

There were snickers at that, then Kar's voice. She had entered from the other door. "Officer Thorn, if you have something to say to me, now's the time. If you have a problem serving under me then speak up."

"There's no problem, Kar honey, you can be on top if you want to."

Kar had no time to react as Hal was suddenly there. He grabbed the offender and threw him against the wall. The man tried to struggle, but it was useless, he was pinned in a painful neck hold. "Officer Thorn, I'm going to let you go now. You will remove your weapons belt and badge. You will then apologize to Sub-Commander Glenn.

"You'll spend the next two weeks in the brig for insubordination, then you'll apply for a position aboard the Orca. You're finished on Reacher. I hear any more crap out of you, any of you, I'll have a word with SUVI 20 about your opinion of her captain. You've never fought a SUVI hand to hand, but I have. It's fun, you learn where all the soft spots are in the armor.

"The rest of you, pay close attention. I'm Chief of Security here, I'll choose who I promote and to what station. If any of you have a problem with that, drop your badge and belt then get out." Nobody moved, they hardly breathed. "Jim?"

"I've got no problems here, Hal."

"Say again?"

"I've got no problems here, Commander White."

"Good, you will assist Sub-Commander Glenn as she escorts this moron to the brig. The rest of you get this through your head, Jeannie Sorenson has kept us all alive a dozen times when we'd all have died under any other commander.

"Admiral Sorenson promotes the most able people to positions of authority for one reason and one reason only, they're our best chance for survival. I plan to follow her example, and believe me when I say, shit like I heard going on in here won't get you promoted, it'll get you nothing but trouble.

"You want to get ahead, look to Sub-Commander Glenn as an example of how it's done. An asshole systematically tried to destroy her career, she didn't whine, she didn't complain, and she didn't quit, she just worked harder at her job and got better at it. She got overlooked a few times because of that fool, but in the end her hard work paid off.

"Understand me well, I'll be watching, and the first time I think ... well, you get the idea. Sub-Commander Glenn is second-in-command here. She's also the only buffer between you and me, keep her happy and I'm off your case. Give her trouble, anything less than your all-out best effort, and I'll be all over you like a bad rash. Do we understand each other?"

"Understood, Commander," came several contrite voices.

"Good. Sub-Commander Glenn."

"Sir?"

"Take a detail and escort this man to the brig. Tell Marcus I said to hold him for a couple of weeks."

"Aye, sir. You, you, and you, bring him."

As soon as they were out of the room Hal sighed and relaxed his shoulders. There were still a dozen or more men and women there. "People, we have to sharpen up. You all know me, and I hope you'll trust me to lead you."

"You kept me alive when the grounders invaded the ship, Commander. I'll follow you," said one older officer. There was a quiet round of affirming grunts and nods.

"People, if we're going to be able to do what we need to do there can't be any more disrespect like that. There just can't. Soon there'll be two crews, big ones, and they'll get rowdy, rub each other the wrong way from time to time, there'll be fights, the odd riot, etc.

"We, as a team, have to watch each other's backs, respect, and protect each other. I need you all to work with Kar. I know her, work hard for her and she'll go to the wall for you every time. Give her less than your best and we'll all fail."

"We'll work with her, Hal," sighed another man. "You're right, the survival of our entire species is at stake here. It's our job to keep the peace and stop us from eating ourselves alive. Kar's a good officer, we'll work with her, or I'll crack a few skulls myself."

"Thanks, guys. Look, our department has been stripped bare of our top people. Let's all work together to show them they overlooked the real top guns. Now's our big chance, let's not blow it."

Hal was barely back in his office when Karissa entered. He arched an eyebrow at her as she sank into the chair facing his desk. She sighed then spoke. "I could have handled that."

"I know, but you've had to fight that battle far too often already, besides, it was that crack about Sessas that put me over the edge. Hell, she's as good a captain as any other. Sheila was captain and I was first officer, but it wasn't long before Sessas was running the show, and with SUVI Twenty to back her up, I'd serve on that ship any day."

"You like her."

"I do, Kar. She's different, yes, but she's sharp, sees everything, instantly recognizes what has to be done and does it, that or orders someone else to do it." Hal smiled. "The thing is, nobody ever thinks to not obey, they just do it."

"Even you?"

"Even me. So, you okay?"

"I'm a little embarrassed, but I'll survive. I should thank you; you kept me from reaching Commander Hoffman's record."

"Oh, you're a long way from that."

"Excuse me?"

"I consulted with the captain and first officer. They agreed to expunge the reprimands that resulted from the false complaints. You've only got one on your record now."

It took her a moment to get her voice to work. "Thank you for that, Hal. That means more to me than you can imagine."

"You got a bad rap, Kar, and nobody caught it. It's over now, now's your chance to shine, so get out there and make me look good to the captain."

She grinned as she rose and saluted. "Aye, Commander, I'm on it." There was a new spring in her step as she walked out. Hal White would never regret promoting her, she'd see to that.

Hal sighed and settled back in his chair. "Okay, I've pissed in the corners, got the crew on side, and my second is secure and on side as well. Yep, starting to think I got a handle on this thing at last.

"Now for the next step; time to piss off the new captain of the Orca. This isn't going to be any fun at all."

Hal reached for the interoffice comm. "Ebony."

"Here, sir."

"I want a full staff meeting in the training area first thing tomorrow. I want every security member plus all the trainees there. Everybody."

"Sir, Captain Singh has that space booked for tomorrow."

"I know. Here's where you earn your stripes, Pilot. Inform Captain Singh that I have commandeered the space."

"Yes, sir."

Hal sighed and braced himself as the call for a general staff meeting went out over the Security channel. Less than ten minutes later he heard Sheila's voice outside his door. "I need to speak with Commander White."

"I'm sorry, Captain, but Commander White can't see you right now. I ..."

"Child, do not make me do this the hard way."

"Send her in, Ebony, it's all right," came Hal's voice over the comm.

Hal indicated the chair in front of his desk as she entered. She kicked it aside and leaned on the desk. "What the hell's the idea of ripping away my training space? I have to get that crew organized and I have damn little time in which to do it. My crew will be there tomorrow, you can book it later."

Hal stood to face her and leaned his own hands on the desk. "That space is the training space for the security force of the Reacher. I'm Chief of Security for the Reacher and I say what and when things happen here.

"You, ma'am, are captain of the Orca, this is the Reacher. If you have issues with the way I run my department, you take that up with my captain, not with me."

They both locked hard eyes at each other and neither spoke for several moments. Wide-eyed, Ebony, who had followed Sheila in, watched, terrified at what would happen next. Finally, Sheila broke first, a hint of a grin started at her lips, he matched it.

"You really like pushing your luck, don't you, Hal?"

He chuckled and sank into his chair as she retrieved the other chair and sat. "Yeah, I fought a SUVI hand to hand, charged into gunfire with inadequate armor, and now I've pissed off the captain of a war ship. I'd say I'm three for three."

Sheila laughed at that. "All right, Hal, you're trying to make a point. I have to say, you really need to work on those interpersonal skills."

"Lilly tells me that all the time."

"Lay it out for me, Hal, what do you need?"

"It works like this, you're not part of Reacher's crew anymore, neither is Brandon Hoffman, you're Orca crew. This is the Reacher. I'm the head of Security here, but I can't function like this. You walk around flinging orders, so does Commander Hoffman, and these people are accustomed to jumping when you guys bark.

"You've robbed me blind for crew, and I've had to recruit a lot of new people. Over half my staff is new officers, they look to the older officers for clues on how to react. The result? I, and my new second, get no respect at all. Here's an example."

He told her about the incident the day before. Her face reddened as she listened. "All right, I'll take him on my crew, but he's going to have a hard time of it unless he changes that attitude. Hal, I see what you're trying to tell me, in your own delicate way. I get it, what do you need from me?"

She nodded her head as he spelled it out. "Okay, you've got it, Hal. I'll go fill Brandon in, then I'll talk to Rhonda. I think I owe her an apology as well." With that she rose and strode from the room.

As Sheila walked away, Hal rose and followed her to the door, Ebony was still standing there. He took her arm and steered her toward the chair then closed the door. Returning to his chair behind the desk, he faced the young woman. "Go ahead, Ebony, say it."

"You could have spoken to her about that a bit more diplomatically ... Sir."

Hal chuckled at that. "Waste of time, Ebony. I know Captain Singh, served with her for years, the woman is a real force of nature. She practically ran the department when Brandon Hoffman was in charge, then she was promoted to this job, and then became captain of a ship and I went with her as first officer.

"I know her, and yes, I could have spoken to her sooner, and she'd have listened, but the issue would have gotten lost in the madness. Sheila Singh is a powerhouse, and she can get seriously focused. Right now she's utterly focused on getting a crew ready for her new ship, I would be too."

"So you went for the shock effect?"

"Had to. Ebony, this wasn't just about getting Sheila's attention or about pissing in the corners; it was about me in this job."

Ebony thought for a moment. "So, you needed her to see you as an equal, not as the subordinate, a role she's always seen you in. This was about establishing your position, not only with her, but with the rest of her crew, and ours as well."

"Right."

"And that's different from pissing in the corners, how?" His roar of laughter brought an impish grin to her face.

"Ebony, I understood you spent every waking hour in VR for years, yet you seem to have a good grasp of things, everything around you, plus real interpersonal skills. Share the big secret with the boss, what aren't you telling the world?"

"Okay, I'll talk. Gramps thought all I ever did was fighter pilot."

"But?"

"I also spent a lot of time in other programs. Gramps was mad at Dad for allowing me to VR all the time, and he wouldn't listen. The deal with Dad was I had to educate myself, one hour of classes to every hour of fighter pilot. We don't have real schools anymore, especially not in the caverns, just VR."

"Well I'll be damned, I thought you were a lot more than just a VR junkie. What's your specialty?"

"Psychology, like my mom. She tried to help the people of the colony, but First Prime sent her to the surface, said she was useless. Dad kept his mouth shut and stayed behind to protect me. The fevers took him a year later, but I stuck to the bargain anyway."

"Ebony, I'm sorry all that happened to you, but I have to say, I'm glad you ended up here."

"Thanks. Will you tell me something?"

"Sure, what's up?"

"Sir, I get the impression you're mentoring me, grooming me for something."

"Damn, you're sharp."

"So, what is it?"

"Ebony, I got lucky here, I found Kar for a second-in-command. Thing is, if anything else goes sideways and I'm not here, she'll get this job, but ..."

"She'll need a second, that's why you're issuing most orders through me, you want the crew to get used to the idea of me giving orders."

"Ah huh, pretty much."

"But all I do is pass along what you or Sub-Commander Glenn say. I don't make any decisions, I'm still a ..."

"That's where those natural keen insights of yours go to work, watch what Kar and I do, see if you can understand why we do what we do, ask us if you need to, we'll help you. Girl, you have the potential to be a lot more than just a fighter pilot."

"But I'll still get to fly the ship, right?" she grinned.

"Yes you will, and I'll get to be her captain. If we go out, we'll leave Kar here to run things while we're go play."

"I heard that," came the voice behind Ebony. Hal chuckled as he'd seen her come in while they were talking. "So, you confessed all, Hal?"

"No, she dug it out of me."

"Right. What do you think, Ebony, are you up for this?"

"Absolutely, if you guys think I can do it."

"All right, then here's what's going to happen tomorrow when the shit hits the fan," grinned Hal, as he leaned his elbows on the desk.

* * * * *

The next morning all was pandemonium as Hal, Kar, and Ebony approached the training area. Both the security forces for Reacher and Orca were there, trying to find out what was going on, for the doors were locked. Hal fought to stifle a grin as he approached. "What's going on here?"

"You tell me," replied Sheila, giving him a sly wink. "We have this area booked for a training session."

"My apologies, Captain Singh, but I need to address my staff. I'll be ten minutes, fifteen tops, then you can have it back."

There came a great muttering at that. "Be silent," barked Sheila as she rounded on the gathered people. "Most of you are no longer crew members on this ship, the rest of you are. Those of us who are Orca crew live on the Reacher, as she is the home ship, but we're not crew here, we're passengers.

"This is the Reacher, and Commander Harold White is Chief of Security here. He controls who has access to security areas and who doesn't. Right now, we don't. We will stand here quietly, and patiently await the commander's pleasure."

Hal unlocked the doors and stood beside them as his officers filed past him, none making eye contact with him or Captain Singh. When all were inside, Hal turned to Sheila. "I'll be quick as I can, Captain Singh."

"Thank you, Commander White. We'll wait right here." As he disappeared inside, she turned to her people. "Listen up, from now on, get it through your heads, you're not crew here anymore, you're passengers. You move your quarters to passenger quarters, you eat in a passenger mess, and more. You no longer have crew privileges on Reacher." By the look of surprise on some of her crew's faces, she knew this clarification was necessary, that Hal was right.

Inside, Hal gave his people a pep talk, read them the riot act about disrespect for superior officers, then another pep talk about teamwork.

"Now, people, we have the toughest job of all. A lot of our former teammates have signed on with Orca, they're no longer crew here, that means no going easy on them, and no special favors. I know many of you have looked to some of them for guidance and leadership in the past, but that's in the past.

"We're a new team, get to know each other, treat each other with respect, and learn to work together. Dismissed."

They rose and filed out, chatting among themselves as they left for quarters or to their day stations. Sheila marched her people in, making a point of thanking Hal for the loan of his space. He grinned as he walked away.

* * * * *

Later that day, Sheila met Ernel at the mess where she was chatting with several of the other Earalithians. The others rose and left as Sheila arrived. She looked up at Sheila and smiled. "Well, how did it go?"

"Worked like a charm," replied Sheila. "I didn't mean to drive away your friends."

"You didn't, my most cherished, they were just keeping me company until you arrived."

"Antha still thinks you spend too much time alone?"

"She does, but she is pleased that I'm so much happier now. So, back to your acting career this morning, Commander White was pleased?"

"Oh yes, he was. That was all my fault anyway, I'm just so used to barking orders in Security that it didn't occur to me that I was undermining him. He's always been there beside me to back me up, I just didn't think this through. I apologized to Rhonda too, because I'm sure the same thing was going on there.

"I ordered my new crew to move their quarters into the passenger areas of the ship."

"Oh?"

"We're not crew of Reacher anymore, we're Orca crew now. When we come home to Reacher we're passengers here, and it's time we started acting like it."

"Does that mean we're moving our quarters?"

"Yes and no."

"Explain please, oh enigmatic one."

"I talked to Moira today. She says they have the captain's quarters and the bridge ready for us. We'll be moving onto the Orca in a few days from now."

"So soon?"

"Oh the ship's not ready yet; we're a long way from that, but we can start moving some of the crew over, giving them hands on training. Here's the plan, the bridge crew will move over, then as we're ready, more departments will move over, one at a time. When we're finally ready to fully man the ship, we'll assemble everybody on the planet then transport them officially to the Orca. It'll be a great show for the folks on the Reacher. In the meantime, we'll all be claiming quarters on the passenger decks for leave use."

"Wow, sounds like fun. So, is that why Admiral Sorenson has been missing for so many days?"

"Missing?"

"My friends are commenting on it, Vice-Admiral Drake is visible, going here and there about the business of running the fleet, I expect, but no one has seen the admiral for many days."

Sheila chuckled at that. "Yes, she's been staying on the Orca, pacing about, looking impatient."

"A psychological device to make the crew work faster without actually demanding they do it?"

"Probably, but she'll also be looking for possible flaws, difficulties, differences between that ship and this one. Orca was built by an alien race, and we have to adapt partly to her, and adapt the rest of her to us. I'm more than happy to have that keen SUVI mind overseeing the refit."

"Okay, so I have only a couple of days to pack up?"

"Sorry, I'll take a day off to help."

"No, my super captain, I can easily manage this, you see to your ship, our soon-to-be new home. Now, eat up and I'll fetch the desserts. It seems there's a new dessert chef, and she can work magic on the taste buds. Maybe you could coax her over to Orca." Sheila promised to try.

Chapter #7

.

Adjustment Time

Another few weeks went by, in which the crew of the Orca, including the captain, took quarters in the passenger area of Reacher. Once again the upheaval was brought to the admiral's attention. "Captain Moore to Admiral Sorenson. Reacher to Admiral Sorenson, please respond."

"Sorenson here, what's up, Rhonda?"

"The passenger representatives are here in my office requesting a meeting with you and the captains of the fleet."

"Can it wait until this afternoon?"

Rhonda glanced at Miriam Holbrooke who nodded. "It can."

"Then I'll call the meeting for 1300 hours. Your briefing room available?"

"Aye, Admiral, it will be."

"See you then." With that Jeannie was gone, but soon Amanda's voice came over the comms. "All captains to the briefing room of the Reacher at 1300 hours. Repeat, all captains to the Reacher's briefing room, 1300 hours. Passenger representatives to the bridge briefing room, 1300 hours."

* * * * *

"All captains and passenger representatives present, Admiral."

"Thank you, Mandy. All right, Miriam, let's hear it."

"Admiral, why have you dumped half the fleet into passenger quarters, and what am I supposed to do with them? Am I expected to represent them as well? Can anybody tell me what the hell is going on?"

"Good questions all," replied Jeannie. "Anybody here care to address this?"

"I'll do it," chuckled Rhonda. "A couple of weeks ago, a situation developing on Reacher became clear. A large number of Reacher's crew has been seconded to the Orca; this you know. What soon became obvious was, a lot of them were senior crew members, accustomed to giving orders aboard this ship and having those orders obeyed.

"As Captain Singh and her senior staff attempted to prepare her crew for the new ship, conflicts between the needs of the two crews began to arise."

"Conflicts?"

"Unintentional conflicts, Admiral," sighed Sheila. "Brandon and I are so used to handling things here that we forgot our place and caused a lot of problems, both for the new captain of the Reacher and her senior staff.

"Rhonda and I both agreed it was time to clarify a few things, like the status of Orca's crew when on the Reacher. The Reacher is the home ship, but we're not crew here any longer. When we're not on the Orca, we'll be back here, home on leave, just passengers on the home ship."

"So, you decided to move all non-Reacher crew to passenger quarters? I like it, it makes sense. Now, the question of the day seems to be, where does that leave Miriam? Does she, as president of the passenger's association, represent them too?"

"She does," replied Rhonda. "Anything else throws the Reacher's crew back into chaos, wondering who is in command of what, and who isn't."

"It makes sense," agreed Jeannie. "How about it, Miriam, are you up for that?"

Miriam Holbrooke looked to the two men with her then back to Jeannie. "All right, Admiral, we can do it, but how is that supposed to work?"

"I'll call them together and make a general announcement, Miriam. Captain Singh will also make it plain to them. Now, what about the crew of the smaller ships?"

"My crew is all security officers," said Hal, "and as such are still Reacher crewmembers."

Rhonda leaned her elbows on the table as she spoke. "Admiral, the small ships' crews also work as Reacher crew when they're here on the mothership, we've had no issues there, and I don't see any developing. They're fine where they are."

"She's right, Jeannie," said Sheila. "It was me and Brandon causing the confusion, and it was pointed out to us ever so delicately by the commander of EX4. Hal was right, and we also need to find new training facilities. We were just commandeering security space out of habit, but that was messing up Reacher."

"What sort of facilities do you need?" asked Amanda.

"Until we can get onto our own ship, just a big space where we can set up some simulators, hold lectures, etc."

"We've got tons of that in the passenger areas," smiled Miriam. "There are about seven hundred of us rattling around in a space designed for tens of thousands. I can get you an auditorium and more."

"Miriam, I owe you a huge apology," sighed Sheila. "I never even thought to look for the space I need in passenger areas, I just elbowed poor old Hal out of the way until he slapped my fingers. Will you help me?"

"Of course," grinned Miriam, "as your representative on the Reacher, it's my duty to help you. I know just the place if you'd like to take a look at it. It's actually quite close to the new quarters your crew have been assigned."

"Miriam, you're my new best friend," replied Sheila. "As soon as we're done here, I'll grab Brandon and have a look, that is, if you're free to show us around."

"I'm at your disposal, Captain. I'll see if I can get someone from Social Engagement to go with us."

"Social Engagement?"

"They've given us the keys, but they like to keep tabs on the facilities, make sure we play fair and don't get up to mischief."

"Well then, we have a solution here?" asked Jeannie.

"We do," replied Miriam. "I'm happy and thank you all for being so open and forthcoming with us."

"All right then, I'll let you all go, and I can get back to work," smiled Jeannie.

"Back to harassing Moira?" grinned Captain Baris.

"More like working with her, Grandfather. It's about my genetic memory; Moira has been picking my mother's brain on a number of things. I'm starting to think I just might make a decent engineer myself by the time this is all done."

There was a round of chuckles at that, then the meeting broke up. Sheila called Brandon, then followed Miriam back to the passenger areas of the Reacher.

* * * * *

At beginning of second shift the next day, Alli had almost given up, for it had been days since she'd seen Kar in the mess hall. Just as she was about to go off shift, she spotted Karissa enter. Swiftly popping a few of her latest creations onto a plate, she hurried to the counter and prepared the tea.

Kar walked into the mess hall for her pre-shift mug of Earalithian tea and gazed around in wonder. The place almost seemed empty. Reaching the counters, she smiled at the girl who passed her the mug of steaming tea and a bowl of some sort of small biscuits. "What's all this?"

"Your breakfast. You need to eat before a long day." Seeing Kar's puzzled look, she dropped her gaze and reached for the bowl. "Sorry, you don't want it, I'll just ..."

She stopped speaking as, instead of her fingers touching the bowl, they met Kar's hand. "I've seen you working the kitchens lately, but we've never met. Are you one of the passengers?"

"Nope, just a really unremarkable under chef."

"Hey now, none of that. Tell me about these, whatever they are."

The girl was keenly aware she was still holding Kar's fingers in her own. With a self-conscious blush, she released them. "They're my own recipe. Commander Peters is always trying to get us to bring new things into the menu. Head chef never let any of us touch anything before, but the new head chef lets me try out things."

"We have a new head chef? Don't tell me, Sheila stole our chef for the Orca."

"She did."

"We'll be picked clean if they soon don't get that ship in the air. Look, it's really quiet in here, and I have to get to work soon. Can you take a break, come out and sit with me while I try out these biscuits?"

The girl glanced up then blushed again. "Sure, I guess that would be okay." She whipped off her apron then hurried around the counters to join Karissa at the table, sitting across from her.

Kar smiled as she took a small bite. "Mmm, not bad, not bad at all. I could get used to this."

"This?"

"Having the chef get my breakfast ready," she grinned. "So, tell me about the biscuits."

"Oh, they're high in fiber, but lots of carbs and protein too. Energy plus to go along with that traditional tea of yours. It's all good stuff, I promise, but I have no idea what planet the flour originated on."

"Sure tastes good, I'll tell you that. Now you tell me something."

"Okay, what do you want to know?"

"Your name, and will you have dinner with me when my shift is over. I've got to run now, but I'd like to pick up this conversation again later."

"Love to. I'll be here."

"Who'll be here?"

The girl blushed again as Kar grinned at her. "Alli, call me Alli, it's short for Allissandra Morgenstern."

"Alli it is. I'll look forward to it all day, Alli."

"Stop making me blush and go, I'll take care of this," she said, as she reached for Kar's mug and plate. Kar patted her hand and walked away.

Alli delivered the tray to the rack then fairly danced out the door and ran to her quarters. "She spoke to me; she wants me to have dinner with her tonight. Now, what was that Ebony said, be honest and up front with her, that's my best chance here. Okay, I can do it, no more shy Alli; up front Alli, that's the new me. I can do this."

* * * * *

"You're late," said Ebony, as Kar entered the office.

"I'm not."

"Later than usual. Alli finally spoke to you?"

"How do you know about that?"

"I'm a chatterbox, I yak away to everybody. I saw her watching you a few days ago, talked to her a bit, and learned lots of good stuff."

"Oh, do tell."

"Not a chance, you'll have to talk to her and learn this stuff on your own. All I can say is, she's interested. Now, get to work before Hal goes to sleep at his desk."

"Yes, ma'am," chuckled Kar, as she stepped past Ebony's desk and opened the inner office.

"About time you got here."

"I'm still five minutes early."

"Yeah, but you're always ten minutes early. What happened, you meet a new boyfriend?"

"Nope."

"Girlfriend then?"

He laughed as her cheeks pinked a bit. "Shut up, Hal. Mind your own damn business."

"I'm chief of Security, everything's my business."

"Go home or I'll tell Lilly you're having a wild affair with a guy down in Sanitation."

He grinned as he rose to leave. "It looks good on you, Kar. Enjoy it." With that, he walked out.

Kar sighed and relaxed back into the chair he'd just vacated. "Enjoy it, he says, sure, why the hell not? I'll ..." she was interrupted by the comms.

Nine hours, three weeks shift rotations worked out, two check sweeps through the main stations, and one brawl in the passenger area later, a man arrived to relieve her for the night shift. "Go home, Kar, I got this."

"All yours, Temba. I'm already gone."

Her shift over, Kar hurried into the mess to see Alli working closely beside another woman. As Alli spotted Kar, she tapped her friend on the shoulder then gathered up two plates and walked around the counter to a more remote table. The place was nearly empty at this time of night, so they would have plenty of privacy.

"Wow, now this is what I call service."

"I aim to please."

"And you've succeeded brilliantly. Alli, talk to me, what's going on?"

Taking a deep breath, Alli braced herself and spoke. "Okay, I'll talk. I've worked back in the kitchen for years, washing dishes, food prep, etc. From back there you see everything out here, but the people out here don't notice you, not ever. I was attracted to you the first time I saw you, but I'm shy."

"Really?"

"Yes, really, and you have to stop teasing to make me blush or I won't tell you the rest." Kar grinned but didn't say anything else. "Okay, so I was attracted to you, but you hooked up with that guy, and I found somebody else. Time went by and we both ended up single again, but I was a dishwasher, you were security, no hope to meet there unless I started a fight with the chef.

"That's when Orca was found, and everything changed. We got a new chef who promoted me to R&D, research and desserts, as he calls it. You got promoted to Sub-Commander, and we're both single again.

I've been waiting for a chance to ambush you with some of the goodies I've developed. I suppose Ebony's already told you all of this already."

"Nope, darn kid is closed as a clam. Wouldn't say a word, just that she knew you're interested. So tell me, Allie, you're an attractive woman, why me?"

Allie sighed and, with a look of deep compassion, reached across the table to take Kar's hand. "Why not you, Kar? What did that guy do to you to make you automatically ask that, to feel unworthy?"

Kar tightened her grip on the girl's fingers. "A number of nasty things, Alli. Okay, so here we are, both single again, older, wiser, and a lot more cautious. I'm willing to give it a try if you truly want to."

"Want to? I've been stalking you for years, of course I want to." That time Kar blushed, then laughed. Alli squeezed her fingers gently. "You said cautious, I hear you, but I do want to try. Shall we hang out together and see where it goes?"

"It'll go straight to my waistline if you keep feeding me like this."

Alli grinned with mischief. "You know I will."

"I know that's your plan, and it'll work, but ..."

"Right now it's late, and you've probably got an early rise tomorrow."

"Yep, 8:00 am."

"What?"

"I took the short shift this time. One tough day tomorrow then two days off. Can you get a day off?"

"I'll give it my best shot. Now, off you go, you've got to be up early."

Chapter #8

Moving in

Another two months went by and work on the Orca went on unabated. Suvi-jean, Amanda, Moira Duncan, Brandon Hoffman, and Captain Sheila Singh sat in the captain's inner-office on the Orca for their weekly meeting. "Moira, are you certain?" asked Jeannie.

"We've got the crew quarters ready for occupation, Admiral. She's sitting here in orbit quite happily, everything looks good, and all the weapons have been disabled for training purposes; we're certain as can be."

"All right, Sheila, is your crew ready?"

"We've got a minimum crew of six hundred as well trained as possible with simulators. I need to get them aboard the ship where they can actually put their hands on the real thing."

"Alright then, Moira says it's ready, go ahead, move them in. Moira, how is the rest of the ship coming along?"

"We're good, Jeannie. We've learned a bunch here, and once we have Orca in tip top shape, we can make some serious upgrades to Reacher."

"Sounds good to me. How are those engines coming?"

"Sorry, Jeannie, Orca's engines are shot. From what we've learned, the Earalith had better engines anyway, so we're fabricating new engines built on the designs we got from that Earalith battle cruiser we salvaged. We're planning to put them in Reacher too."

"Oh?"

"Jeannie, right now, Reacher has hybrid engines, Human built engines with a few Earalith modifications. They're a lot faster than the originals, but not even close to what the real thing could do. According to the engineering manuals from that battle cruiser, it could have flown rings around Reacher."

"Wow, so, what's our timeline?"

"Best estimate? Orca should be flying maneuvers in less than six months. The refit on Reacher should be done in six months after that. Both ships will have stealth shields, better sensors, more defensive weapons for Reacher, etc.

"I assume you'll also want the small ships upgraded as well, that could take another eight months to complete. Jeannie, I'll do what I can to speed this up, but ..."

"No, Moira, take what time you need, get it right. We've got nowhere in particular to go, and nothing special to do when we get there. The idea is to get it right, make it as close to perfect as we can get. We've got everything we need right here in this system for now. Don't rush it, make it right."

Moira Duncan sighed and settled back in her chair. "Thank you for that, Jeannie. On another note, we'll be up to our ears in good engineers by the time we're ready to move on." That brought a round of chuckles.

Jeannie turned to Sheila. "Okay, Captain, you can move your crew in."

"Thank you, Admiral, but first I want to know what's on the Vice-Admiral's mind."

"Mandy?"

"Not my place to interfere."

Sheila grinned as she replied. "Amanda Drake, I'd be a complete fool to ignore your input. Help me here, what do you know that I should? How would you do this?"

"It's something I learned early from a certain super SUVI. This is a big ship, and you can't be everywhere. There have been a few small issues, a few fights, one brawl, etc. as your crew tries to figure out where all the moving pieces fit.

"I'd suggest bringing the rest of your senior staff, the SUVI, plus your security people over first. Give them time to get comfortable with the ship, then bring over the rest, one or two departments at a time. You've already got your chef and a small staff here getting set up."

"Yes, you're right, Amanda. If they all stampede over here at once it would be utter chaos. Thank you, Vice-Admiral, as usual, once again your keen insights will make my life easier."

"Okay, what did I miss here?" asked Jeannie.

"Admiral, when you first gave me the Retriever, I struggled with it. Neither SUVI 20 nor Sessas were under my direct command, and I was a bit unsure how that was going to work. I asked Amanda for advice as she's the most experienced working with SUVI, she had two on her ship plus a SUVI partner."

Jeannie grinned at that. "I'm curious, what did she tell you, Sheila?"

"She told me to sit back and roll with it, so I did. Within days Sessas had practically taken over the ship, it was running smoothly, so I didn't try to fight it, I gave an order and Sessas made sure it was carried out if I wasn't there, that left Hal free to focus on the Strikers. It worked well. This makes sense, we'll do it."

"Then we have a plan. Now, I'm headed home to the Reacher; I've been neglecting the rest of the fleet, and I haven't seen the inside of our quarters for some time. Take me home, beautiful Amanda."

"With extreme pleasure, my love. A day of rest is long past due for you." Smiling, Jeannie took Amanda's hand and they headed for the launch bay and the waiting F1.

As they settled in for the night, Jeannie sighed with delight. "It's good to be home again."

"I agree, sweetheart. The quarters aboard the Orca are comfortable enough, but this is our home, this is the one place where you can actually relax, so it's safe to rest now."

"I'm relaxed."

"Honey, I can feel the tension in you," breathed Amanda, as she began to nibble gently on Jeannie's ear.

"Mandy, what are you doing?"

"Helping you relax, sweetheart."

"I don't know, now that you mention it, I do feel pretty tense."

Amanda's lips were now working their way along Jeannie's jaw line. "Yeah? What do you suggest I do about that?"

"I have no idea at all," gasped Jeannie, as Amanda's fingers found their way into her uniform. "Just keep doing what you're doing, that might work."

Those exploring lips were now on Jeannie's throat. "You think so? Shall we find out?"

"Oh god yes," groaned Jeannie, as she squirmed around to give her lover better access to her body.

* * * * *

Another few weeks went by, and the last of the Orca crew was leaving the Reacher. "I can't believe we finally got a day off together," said Alli, as Kar held her hand and hurried her along.

"Yeah, took me a while to get them in sync."

"You?"

"I set the shift rotations for Security. Once I had your schedule, I could adjust mine to bring it in line. Had to take a few short shifts, but I got it to work."

"Well, we'd better enjoy it, I get my new schedule next week."

"I know, mine's already in sync with it."

"What??? How???"

Kar laughed as she hurried Alli along. "Security has to approve all stuff like that. Usually it comes in, I hit the approve button, and move on. This time I studied it, worked mine out to match up with you, so for the next six weeks our days off coincide."

"Wow, you're amazing."

"Yeah? You think so?"

"I know so," Alli laughed as she sped along beside Kar.

They entered a small room and stopped. Kar stepped to a control panel and set to work. "You want amazing, wait'll you see this."

Suddenly Kar's comm pinged. "This is the captain. Crewman in the forward observation cone, please identify."

"Sub-Commander Glenn of Security here, Captain. Just doing a routine check."

"You mean watching the light show first hand."

"Yeah, that."

"Enjoy, Moore out."

"Kar?"

"Everybody else will be watching this on the big screens, but you and I will see it for real as it happens," said Kar as she stepped away and gently pulled Alli toward the window, carefully putting her arms around the shorter woman.

Looking out into the dark of space, they could see the planet far below, and the bulk of the Orca orbiting close by. Suddenly there was a flash of light, then another and another. "Wow, this is amazing," gushed Alli as she hugged Kar's arms tighter around her. What's going on?"

"The Orca's crew is transporting up to the ship for the official separation ceremony. Captain Singh had them all on the surface so they could make a big show for everybody. Personally, knowing Captain Singh, I think she's testing the abilities of Orca's transporters, plus the discipline of her crew."

"Wow, what a show, this is awesome." She hugged Kar's arms again then turned to face her, resting her head on Kar's shoulder. "This is nice too," she said as she raised her lips for a kiss.

"You know this window is transparent, the whole galaxy will see you."

"You don't want anybody to see you kiss me?" She almost sounded hurt.

Kar grinned. "No, girl, that's really why we're here, I want the whole universe to see me kiss you."

"So quit stalling and get on with it." Alli moaned with delight as their lips met.

* * * * *

While Alli and Kar were having their first kiss under the watchful eye of the galaxy, things aboard the Orca were hopping. Groups of crew members appeared on the landing pad to be marched away by their department heads, then another group of ten would appear. The whole process was accomplished with military precision, but it took thirteen hours to complete.

Finally it was over. "All crew aboard, Captain."

"Thank you, Brandon. Comms, ship wide."

"Ship wide, aye. Go ahead, Captain."

"Attention all hands. This ship is now in orbit and running on auto. It will remain so for the next ten hours. Find your quarters, get some rest, a meal, and then find your stations. At 0:800 tomorrow this ship will be fully manned. Until now your training has been all theoretical, tomorrow it gets real. Get some rest. Captain out.

"Put her on auto, Emmet, Reacher can be our guard dog tonight," said Sheila. She smiled and left the bridge.

Stepping from the shiny metallic corridor into her quarters was like transporting to another planet for Sheila. Ernel had only been on board for a few weeks, but she'd been busy. There was the sweet scent of a tropical forest and soft bird calls everywhere. The walls were gently moving trees, and overhead were blue skies and a few clouds.

Sheila sighed with pure delight as she stopped to listen to the angelic voice of her lover coming from the next room, singing to herself in Earalith. With a grin of mischief, Sheila called out in Earalith. <Honey, I'm home.>

<Your accent is getting a lot better,> smiled Ernel, as she appeared and kissed Sheila's cheek before shifting back to English. "Did you get them all aboard?"

"We did," replied Sheila, as she sank into a chair. "I've put the whole ship on auto until morning, then we get busy."

"Busy? You weren't busy before?"

Sheila laughed at that. "Okay, okay, but you know what I mean."

"I do. Did you take time to eat?"

"No."

"I thought not, so I brought you a meal. Just a minute." She bustled about for a minute, there was a soft hum of a machine, then she returned to pass Sheila a plate. "Try that."

Sheila's eyes opened wide as she tasted the food, and she gave a soft moan of delight. "Ernel, this is pure heaven, since when do we get food like this?"

"Not the whole crew, but we do."

Sheila moaned again as she savored another bite. "Explain."

"My most cherished, you said that, unlike the custom on Reacher, you wanted to open the captain's mess for you and the senior staff plus guests as the occasion arises. I took the liberty of recruiting a chef for you."

Sheila finished and handed back the empty plate. "Give that chef my compliments, that was amazing. So who did you get, and where did you find this treasure?"

"It's a bit of a story, really."

"I'm listening."

Smiling brightly, Ernel came and snuggled into her arms. "Well, I was talking to Antha about it, and she said she had just the man for the job. His name is Karl Ellay, and he was once the head chef for a starship, but when the five original ships got blended, he ended up in Sanitation. He tried to run the department like he did a kitchen, but that didn't work out so good; he got demoted, then retired early.

"He's been seeing Antha for depression, and she suggested I talk to him. I found him in a small café in the passenger's area, complaining to his wife about the lack of taste in the food. When I told him what I wanted he jumped at the chance.

"I then went to Brandon to get help setting it up as a surprise for you."

"Ernel. You are the most amazing woman."

"Oh? Tell me how amazing I am," grinned Ernel, snuggling deeper into Sheila's embrace.

"The home you've created for me here, the gentle way you nurture me, the lengths you go to make my life better ... I have no words to express how much I love you."

Grinning, Ernel shifted back into Earalith. <Then stop talking and kiss me.>

<With extreme delight, my most cherished.,> replied Sheila, pulling the tiny woman closer.

* * * * *

A few weeks later the Reacher's briefing room was abuzz with soft conversations as the gathered people waited for the Admiral to arrive. Finally, Jeannie breezed in with Amanda. Rhonda grinned as she called the room to order. "Looks like we're all here at last, people. Admiral, fleet captains, and Reacher's senior staff are all present."

"Thank you, Captain Moore," said Jeannie, as she sat at the head of the long table. "My apologies for being late, but there was a rumor aboard the Reacher, and I had to investigate."

"You were in the mess, weren't you?" grinned Linsey.

"Indeed we were."

"Was I wrong?"

"No, Linsey, your report of the new dessert chef's talents was a bit conservative if anything. The woman's amazing. So, down to business, Captain Volkov, report."

"All's well with the Recovery ships, Admiral. We've been mining from the derelicts for months now and still have more available. Both ships are functioning perfectly, both crews have become extremely efficient."

"Then I'm happy. Linsey, report."

"Admiral, I've gathered a wealth of information, over thirty new languages for the database, and now expect the universal translator to be a lot faster and more accurate. Engineering is working on downsizing it. We're hoping to get it down to the size of the comms."

"Amazing as usual, Linsey. Sessas, report."

"Ship good, crew good, happy, fly patrols, maneuvers, search skies, all good."

"Search the skies?"

"Always search, watch for danger, new things coming. Reacher watch, Orca watch, we watch. More eyes see more things."

"Indeed they do. Well done, Captain Sessas. Captain Morthel, report."

"EX2 is fit and ready, Admiral. We've been flying patrols with Retriever, maneuvers, and as Captain Sessas says, watching the skies for anything new that might be of interest or a danger. My four crewmen have returned from Orca as has our botanist. EX2 is back to full crew."

"Excellent. Hal?"

"EX4 has been going out to fly maneuvers with EX2 and Retriever. It took a while, but the rest of my crew has finally adjusted to the abilities of our new pilot. Said pilot won't let me fly the ship, says I'm too slow. We're all good on EX4."

"The pilot won't let you fly the ship?"

"Jeannie, until Ebony came along, I held the record for the VR game, fighter pilot. I have to say, she can make that ship move. We all use anti motion sickness meds now."

"You could have her restrain herself a bit."

"No, ma'am. If we ever end up in a combat situation, I want her at her best, and I want the rest of us to be functional. We'll use the meds, it's all good."

He was grinning and Jeannie chuckled at that. "All right, Hal, makes sense. Sheila?"

"Aye, Admiral. Orca now has a full crew aboard, and fully trained. We brought the weapons back on line yesterday and not one casualty has resulted. As soon as we get our new engines, we'll be ready to start test flights.

"Also, it appears that I don't need as big a crew as the original. Orca carried one hundred small two-man fighters, but I only have the fourteen we salvaged from the Wrax. I have two crews per fighter, all trained and flying maneuvers daily.

"I do, however, have one small issue I'd like some feedback on."

"Oh?"

"There's been a few grumblings about me having Ernel aboard, but no one else was permitted to bring their companions. Amanda, what do you think, what do the rest of you think?"

All eyes turned to Amanda. "Orca doesn't have the facilities Reacher does, so, a stint on Orca could be boring for most people, others will have jobs aboard the Reacher that they won't want to give up. Having said that, I see no harm in it, and possible some good.

"Here's what I'd suggest, they maintain their quarters aboard the Reacher as their primary home, but accompany their companions to Orca to test it out. A few weeks of sitting alone in smaller quarters all day waiting for someone to get off shift should sort it out. Some will enjoy it, and others will come home.

"It'll be up to the couples to work it out for themselves. However, you have no way to accommodate children, so couples with children will have to reconcile themselves to some periods of separation."

"That was always the lot of military families on Old Earth," said Olga Volkov. "I think Amanda's idea could work."

"So do I," agreed Sheila. "I'll have Brandon set it up when I get back."

"All right, now we're down to the basics," said Jeannie. "Moira, report."

"Orca is ready as it can be, except for the new engines. They'll be ready by the end of the month, another two weeks to get them installed, then Orca is finished. I'll shift my focus then to the upgrades for Reacher."

"Any estimates on the timeline?"

"It'll be a lot faster, Jeannie. We've already got all the designs worked out, the metals are already in production, so I'd say three months, then another two to upgrade the small ships. Actually, if you're in a hurry to leave the area, we could refit the small ships while Reacher is interstellar."

"No, Moira, let's do it here, then build up a supply of materials to carry with us, just in case. Now, about that other project."

"Aye, well, I haven't had a lot of time to look at it, but, yes, I think we can do it."

Noticing the looks around the table, Jeannie nodded, and Moira went on to explain. "The Admiral wants us to make a few improvements on the Wrax fighters, then build a few dozen more for the Orca."

"Improvements?"

"Yes, Jake, the new stealth shields for example, plus better defenses for that blind spot from behind," said Jeannie. "All these things are strictly for defensive purposes. I'd far rather trade with, exchange ideas with, and help any new races we might meet. Orca and the small ships are purely for defense, not aggression.

"We traded with the Morar, didn't take the ship they had, even though we could have. That's how I want us to proceed. This must be understood by everyone, crew, and passengers alike. We will defend ourselves with everything we've got, but we will not become aggressors.

"So, Captain Moore, report."

"All quiet on the Reacher, Admiral. Since the crew of the Orca shipped out, the Reacher almost feels empty. Miriam reports that the passenger area is boring as hell now."

"Rhonda, I know we robbed you blind for crew," smiled Jeannie. "You've got a lot of untried and new recruits on your crew. How is that working out?"

"Better than I'd expected, Admiral. We're training and drilling them on the job, and it's working out well. There have even been a few bright surprises, as you've so recently discovered."

"Explain."

"When the chef left for Orca, the next man in line moved up. He took one of the dishwashers, put her in charge of R&D, research and desserts. Hal then sent his second to romance the girl, so she'd want to stay with us and not run off to the Orca."

Jeannie laughed heartily at that. "So, all's well aboard the Reacher?"

"It is, Admiral, but we're getting stale just hanging here in orbit. As soon as we've finished the refit, I'd like to fly a few test flights, do a few maneuvers; you know, get the crew back up to form for interstellar flight."

"Agreed, Rhonda. As soon as all the refits are done, we'll run a few joint exercises to fine tune things before we go exploring. Well then, since everything is running smoothly here, I'll take all the SUVI aboard F1 and go over to Orca for a family dinner. It's been weeks since we've had a chance to gather. Dismissed." With that she rose and left the room.

* * * * *

While Jeannie gathered the SUVI for a family get together, Alli sat glumly, staring at the message on her device. "Why so sad?" asked a deep male voice.

Alli looked up to see a man in a security uniform sit across from her at the table where she was waiting for Kar. "Oh, it's a personal matter. I'm waiting for someone."

"Easy girl, I'm not hitting on you, just wanted a bit of company while I eat. I'll move on."

He started to rise, but she stopped him. "No, sit, it's okay. Sit."

He sank back onto the chair. "Thanks."

The man continued to eat his dinner but didn't try to make conversation. Finally she broke the silence. "Can I ask you a question?"

"Ask away. What's on your mind?"

"If you suddenly found yourself in a new job, with a new love interest, but an even better job offer came along on the Orca, what would you do?"

"Two years ago I'd probably have said jump at it. You're young, make that career move, grab that opportunity while you can."

"And now?"

"And now, after a few truly enlightening experiences, I offer you this. What do you really want? What makes you happy? Forget the new relationship for a moment and think about what you want, where you want to go in life, what brings you to your happy place?"

"Wow, that must have been a tough two years."

"It was educational, that's for sure. So, what's your name?"

"Alli."

He smiled as he finished his meal and rose to go. "I'm Marcus. Thanks for the company, Alli. Be good to yourself." With that he walked away.

A moment later Kar joined her. "Was that Marcus I saw you talking to?"

"Yeah, that was his name. Why, are you jealous?"

"Maybe. Was he trying to steal my girl?"

Alli smiled at that. "No, he just wanted company while he ate. I'd been waiting for you, and he came to sit with me. We talked for a bit, that's all."

"I was teasing, Alli. Honest. I'm not trying to own you or hog all your time; I know you have friends."

"Sorry, old reaction."

"It's okay. So, what's bugging you?"

"How did you know ...?"

"It's what I do, honey. I notice when there are changes in normal patterns. Normally you're smiling, upbeat, always trying to lift my spirits."

"Oh god, Kar, I'm so sorry, I ..."

"Alli, Alli, stop now, girl. This is the good part for me. This is where I get to be a support to you too. Look, if it's a personal matter, I don't need to know, I just ..."

"I've been offered a job on the Orca."

Kar sat back, a bit startled. "Oh? I thought you were all pumped about this job."

"I am, I was, I am."

"But?"

"This is a chance to work with a master chef. This guy was the head chef in the captain's mess one time. Captain Singh has him in that job on the Orca now. She loves my desserts, so he's offered me the job there, offered to teach and mentor me for his position when he retires a few years from now."

"And you shared this with Marcus?"

"I don't know what to do, Kar. We're all new and I don't want to be away from you for such long stretches, and I do love my job here, but this is a real opportunity. I'm a bit messed up about it all."

"I'm curious, what did Marcus tell you?"

"He said to focus on what really makes me happy, what do I really want out of life, what makes my world turn. He really wasn't a lot of help."

Kar smiled and patted her hand. "I think he gave you great advice. Know this, I'll be thrilled if you decide to stay here, and I'll be thrilled for you, and support you fully if you decide to take a shot at it."

Alli sighed and gazed at her hands. "You're no help either," she sighed. Kar smiled and patted her hand. Lost in her own indecision, Alli completely missed the resignation in Kar's eyes.

Chapter #9

Orca Rising

Another two weeks passed, and the big day finally arrived. They stood on the bridge of the Orca, the excitement almost palpable. "Moira, tell me good things."

"Aye, Admiral," chuckled the Chief Engineer for the fleet. "New engines installed, tested, and ready for action. Starship Orca is ready for service."

"Now that's what I've been waiting to hear. Captain Singh, the ship is yours. I will now retrieve my people and leave you to it. As soon as you're ready, make a short hop to the next system and back to test both your ship and crew. We'll stay behind and continue our salvage operations."

"Aye, Admiral, and thank you." Sheila was grinning with delight as Jeannie and the last of the repair crews left aboard F1 and Recovery Two. Once they were well away, she turned to the Earalithian man standing at the engineering station.

"Chief Engineer Dorind, is the ship ready for flight?"

"Ship is ready for flight, Captain."

"Good to know, helm, set course for the Morar System, maximum speed."

"Morar System, aye. Course laid in, star drive online, Captain."

"First Officer, is the ship ready for interstellar travel?"

"Ship is locked down and prepared to sail, Captain."

"Helm, hit it." With a slight shudder the Orca vanished from the system, hurtling through the void at heretofore unimagined speeds. "Emmet, estimated time of arrival?"

"Estimated arrival in three days, Captain."

"Three days?" grinned Sheila. "That's double Reacher's best speed so far."

"Indeed it is," he replied, matching her grin.

"Well then, since the excitement is over, I now leave you to it. I'm off to the mess to see if that new dessert chef has invented any more ways to expand my waistline." She smiled to hear the chuckles behind her as she left the bridge.

* * * * *

"Well, they're on the way," said Amanda, as the Orca vanished from the Reacher's sensors. "Moira says they should be back in seven days or less."

"Seriously? When can we get those new engines on my ship?"

"Moira's already working on it, Rhonda," smiled Jeannie. "Apparently the engines are nearly built. Two or three months from now you can match that speed, then we'll top up our supplies and be ready to move on."

"Good to know, Admiral. Am I going to get my chief engineer back, or are you planning to keep her for the fleet?"

Jeannie chuckled at that. "No, Rhonda, you'll get her back as soon as this salvage operation is finished. I may need to borrow her again in the future, but for the most part, she belongs here on the Reacher."

"Music to my ears, Admiral."

"New guy not working out so well?"

"No, actually, he's doing fine, but I think he'd be happier going back to tinkering rather than running the department."

Amanda smiled at that. "Tell him to hold on for a few more weeks then he can go play again."

"He'll be thrilled to hear it. Now, since there's nothing of note going on at the moment, care to join me at the mess for a snack?"

* * * * *

While the captain and Jeannie went for a snack, Ebony was concerned for her friend and mentor, Karissa. "You all right, Kar?"

"I'm good, Ebony. Why do you ask?"

"You've been working overtime every day for weeks. What's up?"

With a deep sigh, Kar leaned back in her chair. "Alli decided to take that job on the Orca. I'll admit I'm a little bummed out about it, but ..."

"Since that guy tried to mess with your career, you wouldn't say a word, tell her how you feel because you didn't want to mess her up like that."

Kar nodded and smiled. "Yeah, I didn't want to hold her back, but I sure do miss her."

"I get that. Kar, you're a good woman, and if it's right for you both, she'll come back to you."

"And if she doesn't then she wasn't the right one in the first place?"

"Yeah, that, or something along those lines. Shift's long since over, want to head to the mess for a tea and snack?"

"Thanks, but I'm okay, honest."

"Okay, I'll shut up and mind my own business; just remember to eat once in a while. You can't keep avoiding the mess and survive."

"Yes, Mom, I promise I'll eat all my dinner, now go away."

With a laugh, Ebony fled the office and headed home. She had a new VR program to explore, effective leadership. With luck she could squeeze in a bit of fighter pilot practice before her grandfather got home.

* * * * *

Three days later, as Kar sat to a lonely dinner, the Orca dropped out of hyper speed to see the Morar system on the sensors. "Shields."

"Shields, aye. Shields at maximum, Captain."

"Sensors?"

"Nothing unnatural moving except us, Captain," came a woman's voice.

"Good to know. Commander Jones, status?"

"Ship all sound, Captain, sensors are clear, speed reducing. We should reach orbit around Tarion in forty-seven minutes."

Sheila grinned with delight. "How's our time over all?"

"Approximately seventy-one hours total should put us in orbit, Captain."

"Just under three days, the admiral is going to love this."

A short while later they reached orbit over Tarion and hailed the planet. They soon got a response.

"Visitor ship, where are you? Please identify."

"Drop shields."

"Shields down, Captain."

"This is the Orca, Sheila Singh commanding. Is that you, Ka'Ron? Can you see us now?"

"Yes, it is I, Captain Singh, we see you now. The Orca? What has become of the Reacher?"

"The Reacher is on another mission. Orca is a ship we found and refitted. We needed to test the engines, so we came to say hello. How are things on Tarion?"

"All is well here, Captain. Captain, is your ship armed?"

"It is. What do you need?"

"There is a meteor cluster that Tarion will soon pass through. Most will burn up in the atmosphere, but there is one large one that gives me concern. Your sensors will be in a better position to gather solid information. Could you take a look for us?"

Sheila looked up to see the woman at the sensors nodding. "I have the cluster on sensors, Captain. That big one could do a lot of damage if it makes a direct hit. Calculating trajectory now. Yes, looks like it will make contact."

"Thank you, Sensors. Ka'Ron, you were right, that big one could be trouble. Shall we go and test our weapons, see if we can make it a bit smaller for you?"

"If you could, Captain, you would have our eternal gratitude."

"We're on our way," replied Sheila, as she pointed at the helmsman. She felt the slight shift as Orca reoriented toward the meteor cluster.

"Sensors, any signs of life on any of those meteors?"

"None, Captain."

"Ver good. Gunner, target that large meteor, you may fire when ready. First Officer, prepare to deploy small fighters."

"Aye, Captain." Even as he relayed her order the gunner fired. A single oscillating beam of hellfire lanced out and sliced the meteor to pieces.

"Gunner, use your smaller weapons now, take out as many of those rocks as you can, but don't shoot our poor little fighters."

"Aye, Captain," he chuckled. "Avoid shooting fighter ships."

"Launch fighters."

"Fighters away, Captain."

Like a nest of angry hornets, the small ships boiled out of Orca and attacked the offending meteors. Soon any meteor of any size was reduced to rubble. Sheila grinned as she watched the exercise over the sensors. "That should do it, recall fighters."

"Recall fighters, aye. All fighter ships stand down and return to Orca."

"Stand down weapons, Gunner."

"Standing down weapons. Weapons at rest, Captain."

"Well done, people. It appears that everything works the way it's supposed to. I'm well pleased, both with the ship and her crew. As soon as everybody is back aboard, take us back to Tarion."

"Aye, Captain."

The fighter bay doors closed and Orca swung around then swiftly returned to Tarion. "Orca calling Tarion."

"Ka'Ron here, Captain."

"We took the liberty of testing our weapons on your meteor cluster. There's nothing left there to give you any trouble."

"Captain Singh, you have our gratitude. Please convey our greetings to the admiral when next you see her. Perhaps we'll be able to fly with you one day."

"Oh? Are you refitting your ship?"

"It's a work in progress, but we have hopes of eventual success."

"Then I'll convey your greetings to Admiral Sorenson and wish you success in your endeavors. Farewell."

"Farewell, Captain Singh. May Orca ever fly true."

Smiling, Sheila turned to Brandon Hoffman. "Are we ready to sail, Brandon?"

"All fighters returned and secured. Orca is secure and ready to sail, Captain."

"Emmet, take us home, all possible speed."

"Heading home, aye. Helm?"

"Course laid in, star drive online and fully charged, Commander."

"Engage drive."

The Orca vanished from the Morar system, hurtling back to where they'd left the Reacher. Three days later they found her hanging in orbit right where she was supposed to be.

"Admiral Sorenson to Orca."

"Orca here, Admiral."

"Welcome back, Sheila. That was a fast trip. Report."

"The Orca and crew performed above expectations, Admiral. We arrived, checked in with the people of Tarion, tested our weapons system on a meteor cluster, then returned."

"Six and a half days in total, Sheila. Moira will be thrilled, as am I, with the speed of the new engines. I'll call a meeting of the captains for 0:800 tomorrow. We can do some brainstorming."

"Acknowledged. If all is well here, I'd like to rotate some of my crew home to Reacher for shore leave. It's been weeks since I've loosened the gates."

"I'll warn Rhonda they're coming. Sorenson out."

* * * * *

"Looks like someone's excited about shore leave," smiled Ernel, as she saw Alli hurrying toward the transporters.

"I am, Ernel. It's been weeks and weeks, and I haven't had a single message from Kar. I'm hoping she's not mad at me or got a new girlfriend, or ..."

"Relax, my young friend, relax. You've got three whole days to get it sorted out. Go on now, scoot."

Nervously wringing her hands, Alli headed for the transportation room. She arrived back on the Reacher with six others in a group. They soon went their separate ways as they hurried off to their quarters or to meet friends and family. Alli arrived to find she couldn't access her quarters.

"Computer, unlock quarters, Ensign Allissandra Morgenstern."

"Quarters unlocked."

"Really? Then why can't I open the door?"

"You are in the wrong location. Ensign Morgenstern is no longer a crew member of Reacher; her quarters have been relocated to passenger quarters. Sending location to comm unit."

Alli stomped her foot in frustration as she turned and hurried off to the passenger areas. Once she arrived, she found everything she'd left behind in her new quarters, but it wasn't home, not her cozy rooms as she remembered them. This just felt cold and empty. She threw her kit on the bed and fled to the mess.

Hours had passed and Alli sat stirring her spoon in a half empty cup of cold tea. "Excuse me, what are you doing here? This is the crew mess, the passenger mess is back that way."

"What??? Oh, hi, Ebony."

"Hi stranger," smiled Ebony as she sat across from Alli. "So, how's life in the new super job?"

"Between you and me, it bites."

"Excuse me?"

"The guy said he'd teach me, mentor me for his job, but mostly what he does is yell at me and makes me do all the jobs he doesn't want to do. I almost never get to try out new stuff anymore."

"Yeah, doesn't sound like much fun at that."

"Have you seen Kar? I haven't heard from her and was hoping to see her here."

"Sorry, she's out with EX4. They've gone dark, trying to sneak up on EX2 or Retriever. Good luck with that."

"So, why aren't you at pilot?"

"Commander White sent Gramps; said I wasn't stealthy enough." She giggled. "He might be right about that."

Alli laughed with her, the first time she'd laughed in days. It hit her then how truly unhappy she'd become, and how happy she'd been aboard the Reacher. "I wonder if my old job is still available," she sighed.

Ebony reached over to pat her hand. "There's one way to find out."

"Yeah, I guess. It's just that Chef Ellay is a super chef, I could learn so much from him."

"Is it worth it?"

"What???"

"Look, Alli, you're a genius in the kitchen. I doubt there's anything he could teach you that you can't figure out on your own, and you'd have a lot more fun doing it. Think about it.

"Now, go see if you can get your old job back while I finish my dinner."

Alli rose and walked away, but soon returned, dejected. Ebony gazed at her sadly. "Alli, I'm so sorry, now I have to be a bitch and rub salt in the wound."

"What???"

"You're Orca crew, no access to this mess. I have to escort you back to passenger areas."

"You're joking."

"I'm not. Sorry. Come on, show me the new quarters." As they started away, there was another security officer headed toward them, but Ebony waved him off with an easy, "I got this." He nodded and turned back.

"Ebony, what just happened?"

"Somebody in the kitchen clearly doesn't want you to get that job back and ratted you out."

"Oh for ..."

"How long are you on Reacher?"

"Two more days, I guess."

"Let me work on this."

"Ebony?"

"Look, I know for a fact Kar misses you, big time, so do I, and you're not happy over there. Let me see what I can do to find a way for you to come home and get your life back, okay?"

"You'll do that for me, you'll help me?"

"Sure will."

"Are you going to talk to Chef?"

"Among others, just go relax, check out the fun stuff in passenger areas and let me work on this, okay?"

"Okay. Ebony, thank you."

Ebony smiled, gave her elbow a gentle squeeze, then walked away. Alli watched her go, then turned to go explore the common area and mall closest to her new quarters.

Two days later Ebony was there to see her off as she returned to the Orca. "I've got something in the works for you," she smiled, "but it'll take a few more days to finalize. When do you get leave next?"

"It'll be another three weeks before I can get days off again."

"Can you make it? If not I'll make something up then toss you in the brig until I get this sorted out."

Alli laughed heartily at that. "Don't go to extremes, girl, I'll survive. Just don't forget about me. Ebony, say hi to Kar for me, give her a hug for me?"

"Sure you want me hugging your girlfriend?"

"Behave. Oops, looks like I'm up. See you next time around."

"Hang in there, Alli."

Ebony waved as Alli disappeared from the landing pad. "Damn, now to make an appointment with Miriam Holbrooke," she mused as she walked away.

The next morning Kar was back at her desk when Ebony arrived for work. "Hey there, how was it, being in command of a ship?"

"It was fun, but, how the hell are you supposed to sneak up on EX2 or Retriever. SUVI 13 is on EX2 and SUVI 20 is on Retriever. I doubt even god could sneak up on either one of those two. First day out we came out of the debris field looking for EX2, she was right behind us."

"So, that's my sad story, what have you been up to?"

"Working on a side project in my spare time."

"Oh? Do tell."

"Nope, it's a surprise. I did see someone special who sends you her best."

"Alli?"

"Yeah. I found her hanging around the mess, looking for her old job back, but the position has been filled. She's back on the Orca now."

"Aw dammit, I'd love to have seen her."

"And she you, so why haven't you contacted her or responded to her messages?"

"She was gone nearly a week before I got a message. All it said was, "Super busy, hugs." Kar sighed and looked at her hands. "I just figured she'd started a new life, and I didn't want to hold her back, so I stayed quiet, giving her a chance to move on."

"Did that make you happy?"

"No."

"Her either. Message the girl, tell her you miss her, for pity's sake."

"You think I should? She's not mad at me?"

"Nope. Want me to make first contact, make sure the coast is clear?"

"Would you?"

"Sure, you big chicken."

"Shut up, Ebony. Yeah, you're right. I can walk into a brawl with no fear at all, or take on a guy twice my size, but this scares the crap out of me."

Ebony was grinning. "I'll do it, but you'll owe me a big one."

"I know, and you're going to gloat when you call it in, aren't you?"

"Count on it."

* * * * *

Next morning all the captains, Reacher's senior staff, and Amanda were gathered in the Reacher's briefing room when Jeannie walked in. "All captains present, Admiral Sorenson," grinned Amanda.

"Thank you, Vice-Admiral Drake," replied Jeannie as she winked at Amanda. "Sheila, report."

"We left this system and arrived in just under seventy-two hours. We hailed the planet, spoke with Ka'Ron, who asked us to investigate a meteor cluster making for the planet. We checked it out, tested our weapons on the bigger ones, then said our goodbyes and came home. Ka'Ron sends his greetings and informed us they're refitting their old ship."

"Wonder what's taking them so long," mused Rhonda.

"Education, probably," said Olga Volkov. "Those people are still in a primitive society, first thing he'd have to do is teach them to read the language, then work from there. I expect it'll take them a few years yet to get into space."

"Once we're done here, we could pop by and give them a hand," suggested Jake.

"We could probably get them in the air," agreed Moira, "but then we'd need a few years to train their crew, especially engineers."

"Let's get back to our own issues," said Jeannie. "We can discuss Ka'Ron's people later. Right now I want to know where we are with the Reacher's new engines. Rhonda?"

"I'll pass that off to Chief Engineer Duncan. Moira?"

"Ten days."

"Ten days?" asked Jeannie.

"We've got the engines built. Tomorrow we'll move them into position for the change. It'll take another few days to make a clear plan of action and double check the numbers. Once we're ready, we'll shut down the old engines and begin the process."

"How long will we be without engines?" asked Rhonda.

"Two weeks, roughly speaking."

"All right, captains, we've only got a few days," said Jeannie. "I want full scans of this area, make damn sure there's nothing new in the neighborhood, or headed this way, before we take those engines offline. Sheila, while the Reacher is down for the refit, I want the Orca right beside her at all times, sensors on full sweep, weapons at the ready.

"Olga, put the salvage crews at Moira's disposal in case she needs extra hands. Morthel, Sessas, Hal, your ships will be patrolling, Linsey too. I'll send F1 out as well. Our home ship will be vulnerable for those two weeks. We'll take no chances at all.

"So, we have a plan. Is there anything further? No, then meeting adjourned."

As they filed out, Jake stepped in beside Hal. "Got a minute?"

"Sure, my office or yours?

"Mine."

They settled into the plush chairs and Hal sighed. "Okay, what's bugging you?"

"Your aide."

"Ebony? Why, what's she done?"

"The girl's doing a lot of investigating in her off time, poking around in strange places, both crew and passenger areas. She's been seen talking with Miriam Holbrooke, plus in the Social Engagement office, and she was seen in the back kitchen talking with the chef. What the hell's going on?"

"Can't take it, can you?" grinned Hal. "You just can't mind your own damn business and let me do my job. It's driving you crazy, isn't it?"

Jake chuckled at that. "Yeah, it is. I tried to talk Rhonda into giving you this job, but she insisted I do it and put you in Security. So tell the first officer, what the hell's going on?"

Hal sighed and shook his head. "Damned if I know. The kid is tight-lipped as a clam, won't say a word. All she'll say is it's a surprise and we'll all love it."

"So it's driving you crazy too?"

"Oh god, yes. This kid is good, Jake, a real find. She has amazing insights, everybody talks to her, tells her everything, but you can't get a word out of her. She's organized, efficient, and tenacious."

"You're training her for your second?"

"Jeannie keeps building more ships; it's only a matter of time before somebody else raids me for people. Kar would make a good chief of security for somebody, but they damn well can't have Ebony."

"Careful brother. It was talk like that that caused me to end up with two wives."

Hal's roar of laughter brought a grin to his brother's face. "Oh no, Lilly would skin me alive for even thinking that. That is not on the radar.

"However, I now have a great second and another in the wings, so I'm happy. Things on the Reacher are quiet, the girls are basically running the show, and my life is good. I plan to enjoy it while I can, because, as we both know all too well, it won't last."

"It never does," sighed Jake, as he leaned back in his chair.

Chapter #10

New Engines, New Job

Ten days later they were finally ready. "Engineering to the bridge, we're all set here."

"Thank you, Moira," replied Rhonda. "Stand by. Sensors, anything new?"

"Nothing new on sensors, Captain."

"Reacher to Orca, we're ready over here, is there anything new on your sensors?"

"Sheila here, Rhonda, we've got clear skies, you're good to go."

"Thank you, taking the engines offline now. Bridge to Engineering, you have a go."

"Acknowledged. Taking engines offline in three, two, one, engines are offline, bridge."

"Acknowledged. Bridge out." Rhonda sighed and gazed around. She could no longer detect that gentle hum that was always in the background, had been there all her life. It was unsettling. "Does anybody know where the admiral is? I thought she'd be here for this."

"She's out on F1, flying patrols with the others," smiled Amanda as she entered the bridge. "Engines are down now?"

"They are," replied Rhonda.

"Thought so, I couldn't feel them. So, now we wait."

"Now we wait. Was there something you need, Vice-Admiral?"

"How about tea and a snack?"

Rhonda chuckled at that. "Let's go. Anita, the bridge is yours."

They gathered their snacks then sat at a table in the nearly empty mess. "With the Orca crew gone, this place sure is quiet," said Amanda.

"I know," agreed Rhonda. "It was never like this as long as I can remember. Vice-Admiral, can I ask you something?"

"Amanda's fine like this, Rhonda. What was it you wanted to know?"

"Thanks, Amanda. I was wondering why the Admiral didn't offer you the Orca, or my job actually."

"She did," grinned Amanda, "but I turned them down. When Suvi-jean and I were first together I got a promotion and a new job, Social Engagement."

"I remember. That was right after the grounder invasion."

"Yes. I threw myself into that job and as a result, I nearly lost Suvi-jean. I vowed then she would always be my top priority. I couldn't accept the Reacher or the Orca. If I did, the ship would demand all my attention, we'd drift apart, and I'd lose her."

"There are other people who make excellent captains, like you for example, but there's only one Suvi-jean."

"But you were captain of the Explorer. Didn't that cause a problem?"

"Not so much, because I was on Reacher most of the time anyway, but it was always in the back of my mind, and I knew I dare not accept a larger ship."

"And your current job?"

"In this job I can stretch myself a bit, and still spend my days with her, being a support to her."

"Wow, any chance I could clone you?"

Amanda laughed heartily at that. "The key here is to find what truly makes you happy then look for someone to share that with, someone who will appreciate it and you, someone whose happy place is being in your company, being a support to you.

"Look at Sheila Singh, she found that she truly enjoys being in charge, and she's damned good at it. Once she accepted that about herself, a companion appeared who was a perfect complement to that for her."

"Yeah, that worked out well. Lady Ernel is a gifted artist, but that is so far removed from being captain of a starship that there's no possibility of competition between them. I can see how that would work."

"So, feeling a bit lonely at the top, Rhonda?"

"Yeah, a bit. See, I spent most of my life trying to get ahead, advance my career. I thought I'd finally blown any chance of that and was resigned to it when the admiral promoted me to captain. I have to admit, Amanda, this job is my happy place, and I'll do everything in my power to be the best I can be at it.

"However, you're right, it's a bit lonely at the top. I have no one at all I can confide in."

"No?"

"Well, Carla has been doing the big sister thing for me, and I'll confess I have bent her ear a few times. I feel like we've become good friends, and I do need that."

"But you're still single."

"Yeah, that. I guess I'm feeling like it's time to settle down a bit, you know what I mean?"

"I do, but as captain, your possible places to look for companionship are limited."

"Yep, it's Orca crew or the passengers and I don't get a lot of chances to socialize with either of them."

"You know, Linsey told me there's a rumor of a new café opening up soon in the passenger's area. I'll keep an ear out, and when it happens, we can go for a coffee and dessert. It might be a likely place to meet people, and a place to spend some of your off-time with people who don't directly report to you."

"You know, that's not a bad idea at all. At worst I'll get to see more of my ship, see if the passengers are truly happy or not, and maybe even meet a few of the Orca crew when they're on leave. Thanks for the suggestion."

"All my pleasure, Rhonda. Now, sadly, I have a meeting with the captains of the salvage ships."

"And I need to go back to work. Keep me posted on that café?"

"I will, but you could check in with Miriam, she'll have all the goods on it for you."

"Good thought, thanks." As Amanda walked away Rhonda reached for her comm. "Captain Moore to Miriam Holbrooke."

"Here, Captain."

"Got a few minutes for me?"

"I'm all yours, your office?"

"How about your office?"

"Tea or coffee?"

"Tea please."

"I'll have it waiting for you."

"On my way." Rhonda was smiling as she headed for the passenger area of the ship.

* * * * *

Later that same day on another ship.

Tired and demoralized, Alli returned to her small room aboard the Orca. Chef Ellay had been in a real mood today, and it had been a long one. The captain and her senior staff had lingered over dinner, discussing the upcoming events as the Reacher's engines had just gone offline, leaving Orca on full alert status.

When they finally broke up the meeting it was late, and Alli had been left to clean up as chef had already gone for the day. Exhausted, she threw herself onto the bed and burst into tears. It was some time before the soft ping of the computer penetrated her awareness. Puzzled, she hit the button.

"Audio message for Ensign Allissandra Morgenstern from Reacher Security Officer Ebony Graves."

"Route to this station. Begin."

"Hey, Alli, it's me. I'm shipping out for two weeks on EX4, but I've got it done. Come on home, then meet with Miriam Holbrooke and Sandra Okomora of Social Engagement. They'll give you the details.

"Okay, okay, I'll talk. There's a small café they want to open, but I convinced them it needed to have something extra special. That's you.

"Bye, see you in a couple of weeks."

Next morning Chef Ellay arrived in the captain's mess to find it spotless, and a message disc on his counter. He hit the button and Alli's image appeared above it. "Chef Ellay, you are the most overbearing and arrogant man I have had the misfortune to meet. If that's what they called teaching and mentoring on Old Earth, I'm glad I was born in space.

"I quit. I swear, if I ever see your face again I'll slap it with a pie."

His mouth opened, but no sound came out for a moment, then slowly, he began to smile, then chuckle. "Young woman, I spoke almost those same words to my first over chef nearly fifty years ago. Good luck, you'll make a fine chef one day." Still chuckling he set to work.

Sheila and Ernel were awake early, Ernel found the message from Alli saying goodbye. Sheila overheard it. "Ellay chased off our dessert chef? Damn, ah well, I guess my waistline will thank him for it, but I won't."

Ernel smiled and kissed her cheek. "You go to work, my most cherished, I'll go see our young friend off."

She hurried away to transport where she found Alli, suitcase in hand, waiting for her turn. "Hey there, leaving without giving me a goodbye hug?"

Alli blushed as she hugged the tiny woman. "Ernel, I'm so sorry, but I just can't ..."

"I understand, Alli, I do. I've heard him shout at you in the kitchen and I admit I've spoken to him about it. He said that was the way he trained as a boy, and that it's supposed to make you able to function under extreme pressure. I didn't believe it.

"Will you be okay?"

"I will. Oh, here, this is for you," said Alli.

"What's this?" asked Ernel looking down at the info stick in her hand.

"The recipes for Captain Singh's favorite desserts. You can make them yourself, but don't let old Ellay see them."

Ernel laughed with delight. "I'll hold them sacred, Alli, I swear it."

"Looks like I'm up. I'll message you when I get settled."

"Promise?"

"Promise." With that Alli stepped onto the transport pad and vanished in a flash of light.

* * * * *

Alli had been back on the Reacher for two days before she got her appointment with Miriam Holbrooke and Ensign Sandra Okomora of Social Engagement. "Come in, Ms. Morgenstern," smiled Miriam.

"Alli, please, call me Alli."

"Thank you, Alli. First, let me say we're thrilled that you'd consider taking this on for us."

"Ebony didn't tell me much about it, except that you want to open a café and want me to work there."

"Hi, Alli, I'm Sandy. We don't want you to work there, Alli, we want you to run it. Actually, it was Ebony who came up with the idea."

"You want me to run it?"

"Yes," said Miraim. "Here's what we have in mind. It's a small, intimate space, not an open mess hall, or a larger gathering place. We want a small, romantic space specializing in a few menu items, but mostly in desserts. You'll have two or three servers and two more kitchen staff to help you. Your task would be to organize it and come up with those magic desserts of yours."

"Oh my god, you're serious?"

"We are," smiled Sandy. "When Ebony cornered me with this idea, I was in the mess choking down something your replacement had concocted. She had me in an instant. I could see it in my mind, a few tables, dim lights, soft music, and a slice of heaven on the plate.

"So, are you up for it?"

"Yes, oh yes, I'm in. When can I start?"

"How about we go have a look at the space right now. You can look it over, make me a list of what you need, and I'll have Stores deliver it."

"Let's go," exulted Alli, as she leaped to her feet.

They left Miriam's office and headed out into the main mall. This was where the theaters, cafes, shops, artist studios, bars, etc. were located. On a quiet corner they came to an empty space. Sandra unlocked it and they went in.

The lights came up as they entered. Alli saw a huge empty space, but her mind instantly showed her what it could be. "We'll need to partition it off, the kitchen over here, washrooms here, we'll have room for about twenty tables. But I'd like to cut that down to fourteen, make more space between them for more privacy, more intimate."

She stopped speaking as she noticed the two women beaming at her. "What?"

"Ebony was right," grinned Miriam. "You're exactly who we want here. Engineering is swamped with installing the new engines, but I have a friend on Recovery Two. I'll see if I can borrow a few of their crew to set this up for you. Give me a minute."

She reached for her comm unit. "Miriam Holbrooke to Chance Morita."

"Here, Miriam, what's up?"

"I've got a job for you and a couple of men; can you help me?"

"Not a problem, Reacher's crew won't let us touch anything anyway. Where are you?"

"Main mall, southeast corner."

"On our way."

"Alli, these guys will get this done for you, and I'll authorize whatever they need to make it happen," said Sandra. "I can't wait to see what you do with the place."

"I can't wait to taste what comes out of the kitchen," said Miriam. "Ah, here comes Chance."

Miriam introduced them, Alli explained what she'd like to see, and with a chuckle of delight, Chance set the crew to work. Sandra stayed with them to see they got whatever they needed for materials. One week later, Alli had her café and was training staff.

* * * * *

Another week went by, then the peace was broken. F1 swept into the cargo bay of the Reacher. The hatch flew open and Jeannie leaped out, racing for engineering. "Moira, tell me good things."

"We're right on schedule, Admiral. Two more days and we'll be running tests."

"Speed that up, something just came through the rift, a ship, but we don't know anything more at this point. The sooner the Reacher has her new engines, the happier I'll be."

She fled toward the bridge. Arriving at a run, she met Rhonda just leaving. "Admiral?"

"A ship just came through the rift, get your people prepared for whatever comes. If it's good news then so much the better, but ..."

"Understood, Admiral. Where will you be?"

"On the Orca with Linsey and Sheila. We'll go out and take a look at it. Crack the whip, get those engines online."

"Aye, Admiral." Rhonda was already talking to Jeannie's disappearing back.

"Sorenson to Vice-Admiral Drake."

"Here, Jeannie, what's up?"

"New ship just came through the rift; we're going out for a look. Find Linsey and meet me at Transportation."

"On it."

Jeannie found Amanda and Linsey already waiting at the transport area. "Orca is waiting for us, let's go."

They appeared on the Orca to be met by the captain. "Welcome aboard, Admiral," smiled Sheila. "Captain to bridge, they're here, take us out."

They felt the gentle pull as the mighty Orca reoriented herself then leapt away from the galaxy. A short hop later they were back near where the Reacher had first come through the rift to appear in this area of space. "There she is, Captain," said the man at the sensors, as he put the new ship up on the forward screen.

"Looks in rough shape," mused Brandon Hoffman.

"Yes it does," agreed Jeannie. "Are we hearing anything from them?"

"Sorry, Admiral, I've got it on the headset," said Linsey. "Just a minute more and, there we go. I think this is it."

Linsey flipped a switch and a voice filled the bridge. "Calling anyone who can hear this, help us, our ship is badly damaged, please help us."

"Go ahead, Admiral, the universal translator should work for you now."

"Thank you, Linsey. Attention, damaged ship, this is the Orca, what do you need?"

"Where are you? Please hurry, we're desperate."

"I detect no weapons, Captain Singh."

"Thank you, Sensors. Lower our shields."

"Aye, Captain, shields lowered."

The Orca suddenly appeared beside the stricken ship, causing further terror to its inhabitants. Jeannie spoke again. "Ship, we're right beside you, what do you need?"

A shaken voice responded. "Engines are down, we're losing atmosphere, power is fluctuating. We have many badly injured people. Can you help us?"

"We'll do what we can for you. Send us the coordinates of your safest landing site." Jeannie turned to Sheila. "I'll need an enviro suit and the SUVI with me."

A short time later they were ready. "Attention, damaged ship, we're ready to transport over."

"Our landing bay doors are damaged and won't open. We can try to get an outer hatch opened manually."

"Unnecessary. We'll transport aboard." At Jeannie's nod she and the SUVI disappeared to reappear on the alien ship.

As they arrived in a flash of light there were sudden high-pitched screams of fright as several creatures fled from them. They were a humanoid species, shorter, with leathery skin and all wearing uniforms of a shiny material. A few moments later, three new ones appeared wearing slightly more elaborate uniforms.

"Are you from the ship, Orca?"

"We are," replied Jeannie, the small box attached to her suit translating for her.

Nineteen was gazing at the instrument in his hand. "Atmosphere is breathable, Five."

"Excellent," said Jeannie, as she and the rest reached up to unfasten their helmets. "Greetings. I'm Admiral Sorenson of the Wandering Fleet. Show me where the need is greatest."

"Greetings, Admiral Sorenson, I'm Captain Grill of the Maccay Exploration Fleet, this ship is the Att't. Right this way."

They followed the captain as he led them through the damaged areas. "We're a curious people, Admiral. May I ask, how large is your territory, how far has your species expanded into this area of space, and how did you get so close to us, our sensors are still functional, yet we couldn't detect you?"

"We're only a few ships, Captain. We were tossed over here even as you were."

Just then they reached the most damaged section. There were several people working to contain the damage, but they were injured as well. "It'll take time to get this rubble out of the way, Captain," sighed one man. "Once we get through, we can access main engineering and stop the atmosphere leaks. He nearly went into shock at what happened next.

The SUVI shed their enviro suits then set to work. The Maccay were astonished by the physical strength of the SUVI. In just a few minutes the damage was moved aside, girders bent back out of the way, heavy objects lifted and shifted, then the pathway was clear.

Jeannie straightened up, flexed her back, then reached for her comm. "Sorenson to Orca."

"Sheila here, Admiral, what do you need?"

"Send over your medics and a couple of engineers to start with. The atmosphere is breathable."

"Understood. Repair crews and medics on the way."

They began arriving in twos and threes. "Admiral Sorenson, I have no words to express my gratitude for your assistance. May I ask, what is your species?"

"Most of our people are human, a few are Earalith, and those of us you have already met, are SUVI. Those now arriving are humans, and there is Dorind, the chief engineer. He is Earalith." They continued their inspection of the ship.

"Tell me, Captain, what do you know of how you arrived here?" asked Jeannie as they arrived back near Engineering.

"Nothing at all, Admiral. One moment we were studying a dying star and the next we were battered and thrown about to appear here, wherever here is."

"We are currently just off the tip of the galactic arm, at least one of them. Ah, here comes Dorind. Dorind, what's the good word?"

"Their engines are badly damaged, Admiral. There's nothing more we can do here. If we can get the ship in close to the debris field they should be able to salvage what they need to make repairs. For now we've got the atmo leaks sealed, auxiliary power stabilized, air and water processors are being repaired. The ship is safe but needs a lot of work."

"Thank you, Dorind. Do what you can for them for now." Jeannie reached for her comm. "Sorenson to Vice-Admiral Drake."

"Drake here, Admiral."

"Amanda, relay a message to Olga for me. Tell her to bring her ships out for a look, see if they can tow these folks in close to the debris field where they can salvage what they need for repairs."

"Aye, Admiral, relaying message."

Jeannie turned back to Captain Grill. "Now, Captain, perhaps we could retreat to your bridge and let our combined people get your ship stabilized."

"Agreed, Admiral. Can you tell me why our sensors couldn't detect your ship?"

"It's our defensive shields, Captain. When we were thrown into this area of space as you were, we encountered a species determined to destroy all other forms of intelligent life. We managed to escape them, but they followed us to the next system.

"Eventually we defeated them, then returned to this system where they'd done so much damage to so many, to make our repairs. While salvaging what we needed we found a hidden warship and converted it to our needs. The Orca is an amazing ship built for war by a peaceful people who understood they needed to defend themselves. When they realized they couldn't defeat the Wrax, they hid the ship for future generations."

The captain suddenly looked as though he'd been shot. It took a moment for him to regain his breath. "The Wrax? They're here?" he asked in a shaken voice.

"No longer," replied Jeannie. "Tell me what you know of the Wrax."

"They were an ancient race of destroyers, long since vanished by the time our people returned to the stars. Originally our people were explorers, but the Wrax came and decimated us, only a few remained to repopulate the planet. Eventually we renewed, re-discovered the ancient knowledge, re-educated ourselves, built new explorer ships, and returned to the stars.

"We found the Wrax had gone, vanished into decay and the passage of time. The wreckage and destruction they left behind littered our sector of space. So many destroyed civilizations we explored, but we found no life except our own. It seemed we were the sole survivors of the Wrax Expansions. If they're here we must flee as fast as possible."

"They're no longer here. A single Wrax ship was thrown here even as we both were. We destroyed them and their ship. You have nothing to fear from the Wrax in this system, however, the destruction they left behind will provide you with much useful material to make your repairs."

"Thank you, Admiral. In our explorations we discovered many archives of knowledge, buried and hidden from the wrath of the Wrax. They saw themselves as the only species worthy of existence and sought to destroy all others. They were quite successful for centuries, but eventually disappeared."

"As do all aggressive empires, first they expand, then they rot from the inside. Ah well, not our problem."

"Admiral, may I ask what you will do with us?"

"We'll try to get you close to the debris field where you can make repairs. We still have our own repairs to complete, so we'll be neighbors for a while."

"Can you tell me about this region of space?"

"No, for we have yet to explore it for ourselves. The next system to this one holds the remnants of another species the Wrax tried to eliminate. They fought the Wrax and lost but managed to survive. One of them was instrumental in our final destruction of the Wrax.

"This system, and that one, are all we've managed to explore so far. Once we finish our repairs we'll go further into this region."

"So you're explorers?"

"Yes and no, Captain. You've met each of the three species that make up our diverse people. Our small fleet contains all that is left of each species. We're survivors, Captain Grill. Above all else, we are survivors, hunter gatherers, scavengers, and more, but survivors above all else."

"Then I grieve for your loss, and applaud your determination, Admiral. My own species once faced the same fate, but managed to return, and I'm sure such a determined people as you will also."

"So, you're saying we're all refugees here in this section of space."

"Pretty much," replied Jeannie. "We haven't found any native species as yet, but after our encounter with the Wrax we came to understand we need to be prepared in case we do meet a hostile group. We are so few but were fortunate to discover the Orca. Both that ship and the technology she contained have greatly increased our chances of survival."

"Would you be willing to share that technology with us?"

Jeannie allowed her shoulders to sag a bit. "For the moment I'll say only that it's up for discussion. As a SUVI, I will surely lean your way in this, but the humans can be a bit paranoid. I'll put it before the combined leaders, then take their thoughts under advisement before making a final decision."

"That is only prudent, Admiral, and I would expect no less. That you're willing to discuss it gives me great hope for keeping my people alive and finding our way home."

"For the moment, let's just focus on getting you patched up." Jeannie smiled as she reached for her comm. "Sorenson to Vice Admiral Drake."

"Here, Jeannie."

"Tell me good things, Mandy."

"The salvage ships are here and grappling on to the Att't. Olga says no problem to tow her to the debris field."

"Understood. Let me know when they're ready."

"Olga here, Admiral. We're all hooked on and ready to go. We'll be gentle and go slow. We don't want to do any more damage."

"That's good to know since I'm still aboard." That brought a laugh from Olga Volkov. "In your own time, Olga."

"Thank you, Admiral. We're underway."

The ship gave a gentle shudder as the recovery ships tightened the tow lines. "We'll soon have you safely settled, Captain Grill. Once we arrive, we'll confer with our combined repair crews and decided from there what we do next."

"Understood, and again my gratitude for the rescue, Admiral."

Chapter #11

Tests and More Tests

It had taken several days but the café was ready, now Alli had only to train her staff. She still hadn't seen Kar or Ebony, they were still out on EX4, flying patrols. There had been a bit of excitement when the Att't came through while the Reacher's engines were down, but that soon passed.

The big ships all hung in the sky close to the debris field while the small ships flew patrols, and the café, named Simple Pleasures by the chef, came into shape. "Well, tomorrow's opening day, our big test, and I believe we're ready as can be. Our special guests will arrive at noon, and we have to be set up by then."

"Relax, Alli," smiled the tall woman beside her. "Look, you three have the kitchen under control. Silan and I are ready, excited about getting Simple Pleasures on the map, so we'll be making sure to keep the customers happy. That VR program on customer service that Ebony told you about sure was an eye opener. I learned a ton from it and can't wait to put it into practice."

"Thanks, Maxi. Yes, I'm nervous, does it show?"

"You're vibrating so hard I'm surprised Engineering hasn't sent someone to check it out," grinned Maxi. "Go home, get some rest, then come back and work your magic so we can impress the entire ship with our amazing café."

"Okay, guys, let's lock her up and go home. See you all in the morning."

Alli slept little that night, and she was back in her kitchen early. "Wow, sure smells good in here," sang Tegan, as she entered and started pulling out the bread for sandwiches. "I'm surprised Ivan isn't here already."

"Right behind you, girl. I'll get the soup stock going, you keep at the sandwiches." Alli looked up to see him smiling. "We've got this, Alli, you're on desserts."

"Aye, chef," she grinned as she went back to what she'd been doing, absentmindedly brushing a bit of flour off the tip of her nose with her arm. Noon arrived and she glanced out to the seating area to see Maxi guiding the captain to a table. The entire senior staff was here. She swallowed hard and answered the soft alarm from the oven.

Out in the main area, everyone was finally seated. "May I have your attention please. Captain Moore, President Holbrooke, senior staff, my name is Maxine Thorne, Maxi, and I welcome you all to the world of magic we call Simple Pleasures.

"Please check your dietary conscience and caloric inhibitions at the door, for we specialize in taking your taste buds to levels of ecstasy they have not reached before. There are menus on each table, so I'll give you a few minutes to look them over then Brittany, Silan, and I will take your orders. Enjoy!"

She stepped away and Alli hid behind the door, listening to the soft buzz of the conversation in the seating area. A few minutes later the girls went back out, took the orders then set about swiftly filling them. Alli spent the next while dividing her attention between listening to the conversations and nervously pacing about the kitchen, wringing her hands.

The captain's groan of delight brought a sigh of relief and a huge grin to her face. A few minutes later Rhonda signaled, and Maxi instantly appeared. "Is everything to your satisfaction, Captain?" she asked with an impish grin.

Rhonda almost blushed as she gazed into those dazzling blue eyes. Finally, she matched the woman's grin. "Yes indeed, everything's perfect. I have to admit, I've never tasted better, and I have a good idea who's back there in that kitchen. Would you ask the chef to come out, please?"

"With pleasure, Captain."

She turned away, but soon returned with Alli in tow. "I thought it was you," smiled Rhonda. "I will admit, I went into mourning when you left the Reacher for the Orca. Welcome home. So tell me, how did you end up here?"

"The job on the Orca was a bust, Captain. Chef Ellay promised to teach me, but all he did was yell at me. I tried to get my old job back, but it had been filled, and then I was tossed out of the crew mess. A dear friend managed to put this together for me."

"Ebony Graves," said Jake, who was at the next table with Carla, Hal, and Lilly. "So this is what she's been up to."

Alli smiled as she spoke to him. "Yes, it was Ebony's idea, but so many others pitched in to help. I'm never leaving home again, I have far too many friends here."

"Thank god for that," chuckled Rhonda. "Alli, is it? Alli, you've outdone yourself; I missed your awesome touch in the mess, and I'm glad you're back to stay. I'll return here often."

"We'll look forward to it, Captain," smiled Maxi, as she returned. Alli glanced at Maxi then back to the captain. She grinned and backed away.

Alli went to each table, and everybody had only high praise for her efforts. She was ecstatic.

As she settled down to sleep that night she sighed with relief. "It went well, it really did. This is so great, gods I can't wait to see Ebony, give her a big hug then feed her until she can't move."

She sighed and pulled her blanket tighter to her chin. "I wonder if Kar will ever come to Simple Pleasures. I hope so, oh gods, I hope she does, I hope we can start over. I really blew it with her, and I want another chance there too." She was still practicing what she'd say to Kar as she drifted off to sleep.

* * * * * *

Two days later it came to pass.

"Captain Moore to EX4."

"EX4 here, Captain."

"Kar, bring your ship in for her refit, Reacher's engines are back online. Oh, tell that pilot of yours that I know what she did, and I want to talk to her about that. Moore out."

Ebony turned around in the pilot's seat to gaze wide-eyed at Kar. Slowly a huge grin spread across her face. "Ebony, what have you done?" came Kar's puzzled voice.

Ebony's grin just got bigger. "Oh yeah, I love it when a plan comes together. I'm betting the captain enjoyed my little surprise."

"You surprised the captain?"

"That and more."

"What did you do?"

"You'll see soon enough."

"Ebony Graves, as your commanding officer I order you to tell me what the hell is going on."

"Nope, sorry, can't talk."

"That's insubordination, Pilot."

"I know. Take me home, put me in the brig. I'll never talk."

"Dammit, Ebony ..."

"Just a bit longer, I promise I'll reveal all as soon as we're back on the Reacher."

"You'd better, or to hell with the record, I'll beat it out of you." Ebony giggled as she turned back to the control panel.

* * * * *

Aboard the Reacher, Rhonda was walking back to the bridge with Jeannie and Amanda. She'd taken them to Simple Pleasures for a dessert-fest. "Rhonda, that was amazing," said Jeannie. "Once Linsey and Eighteen discover that place, I'll always know where to find them."

That brought a laugh from Rhonda and Amanda. "That café wasn't there before, yet I did recognize one of the desserts. What's the story on this?"

"It all started with the finding of the Orca, Admiral. Our chef was whisked away for her crew, and a new guy promoted for us. The new chef promoted a magic worker to R&D, but she too was soon enticed away to the Orca. She was unhappy there and asked for her job on Reacher back, but it had been filled.

"That's where Hal's aide, Ebony Graves, stepped in, she's friends with Alli, our magic chef. She did some fast poking around, twisted Miriam's arm, bullied Social Engagement, recruited a few talented people, and set this all up so her friend could come home."

"This Ebony sounds like a resourceful young woman," smiled Jeannie, "and she sure has added another delight to the Reacher."

"More than one, I'd say," grinned Amanda.

"What do you mean, Mandy?"

"Didn't you notice how that tall girl, Maxi was it, who served us gave Rhonda the eye?"

"No. You know I have no idea how such things work. Tell me all."

"When we walked in, the girl lit up with a bright smile, but her eyes went straight to Rhonda. If I'm not mistaken, Rhonda actually blushed a bit at that point." Amanda was grinning and Rhonda's cheeks pinked a bit at that.

"The woman sure is attractive," said Jeannie. "What do you think, Rhonda."

"I think you two are lucky you out rank me, or I'd toss you in the brig for teasing the captain. Yes, the girl sure is delicious, but ..."

"She's interested, Rhonda, that's easy to see," said Amanda.

"I believe, by the color in the captain's cheeks, that she is interested as well," grinned Jeannie.

Rhonda sighed. "Don't you two have something to do besides tormenting the poor captain?"

"All right, we'll take pity on you, but only because you shared the secret lair of the dessert queen with us," replied Jeannie. "So, to work, I have an idea we need to discuss."

They stepped into the briefing room and settled into the chairs. "Now, Rhonda, tell me what you can of this Ebony Graves, what's her story?"

"She's a grounder. According to her grandfather all she's ever done with her life is play VR games, fighter pilot. Jake recruited him for pilot of EX4 but the man is getting on in years, and only agreed to it if Jake would give the girl a shot at the job when her grandfather retired. Jake agreed if she'd take the security training. She aced it in record time.

"During that time, I got Jake's job during the battle with the Wrax, so I went along with the deal, then I got promoted and then, with the redistribution to accommodate the Orca, Hal got the job. Ebony cornered Hal and he agreed, but she had to become his aide. She excelled well beyond expectations, so he promoted her. He then asked her how she did it, if all she'd ever done was VR fighter pilot.

"She confessed she'd spent all her years in the caverns educating herself through VR programs to become a psychologist like her mother. The mother had been sent to the surface as useless, but the father stayed behind to protect the child. He died of the fever the next year and the girl was left with the grandfather.

"Seeing the girl's potential, Hal's been secretly grooming her as a second, should Kar be snatched away, or should he be promoted, leaving Kar in charge."

"I see," mused Jeannie.

Amanda grinned. "Let me guess, you're thinking the idea of VR training is a good one, and that we need special programs developed for every department, right?"

"As always, my bewitchingly beautiful companion, you see right through me. Yes, that's what I'm thinking."

"And you're going to steal Ebony away for your own staff, aren't you?" sighed Rhonda.

"Steal is a rather harsh word," chuckled Jeannie. "I like acquire so much better."

Rhonda laughed heartily at that. "All right, Admiral, I do like it, a lot. So, the big question now is, who has to tell Hal?"

"I'll do it," smiled Amanda. "He'll shoot anybody else." She rose and headed for the door.

Hal leaned back in his chair, shaking his head. "You guys hate me, all of you. As soon as I find a winner you snatch them away. So, not only will I need a new pilot, but I'll need a new aide as well?"

Amanda chuckled at that. "Oh come on, Hal, you've gotten spoiled with Kar and Ebony running the show for you."

"And that's bad because? Okay, okay, I'll admit it, the kid's got a world of potential. You know, it was all a happy accident for both of us. I agreed to honor Jake's deal but made her tend the desk and fend off the small stuff for me. All I hoped for was a few days to get settled in, and to test her resolve. All she wanted was to pilot the ship.

"The funny thing is, she enjoys the job, and she's a natural leader. She's a real jewel, Mandy, but she's young."

"So were the rest of us when Jeannie started promoting us all to top positions. Okay, Hal, I know, I'll keep an eye out for her and watch her back. She'll be available to you as pilot of EX4, but outside that she'll be working for Jeannie."

"You mean you."

"Me?"

"Come on, Mandy, you're a lot more visible around the ship now than Jeannie, and I assume Ebony will be working mostly aboard the Reacher."

"Yeah, you're right about that. Gee, Hal, thanks for training a great aide for me."

His roar of laughter brought a naughty grin to her face. "Shut up and get out of my office, you thieving Vice-Admiral, you."

It was her turn to laugh. "Hal, if you still need her here, ..."

"No, Mandy, you're right, I am getting lazy. Go ahead, Ebony works her butt off, she'll do you proud."

"Hal, thanks for making this easy for me."

"If I didn't, Suvi-jean would just beat me up again. Go on, Mandy, but you guys owe me one."

"Yes we do," she smiled as she left the office.

Chapter #12

Another New Job

EX4 touched lightly down in the cargo bay and her crew disembarked. They'd been in space for over two weeks while the Reacher got her new engines, and the crew was ready for some shore leave. As they walked away from the small ship, Kar took Ebony's arm and steered her aside. "All right now, talk to me, little sister. What have you done and how am I going to keep you out of trouble?"

Ebony just grinned at her. "Okay, I guess it's time to reveal my big surprise." She took Kar by the hand and towed her along. "Come with me and I will reveal all."

Kar's confusion grew as she realized Ebony was taking her into the passenger area. "Ebony, where are we going?"

"Hush now, we're almost there. It should be around here somewhere, I just need to … ah, that must be it. Come on."

The café was called Simple Pleasures and there was a lineup to get in. Ebony kept a straight face as she elbowed her way through. "Sorry folks, Security here, make a hole, sorry, Security coming through."

When they reached the entrance a tall girl appeared, recognized Ebony then squealed with delight as she hugged her tightly. "Ebony, oh god it's so good to see you. You were absolutely right, this is awesome. Does Alli know you're here?"

"Nope, we just got back and came straight here for a snack."

"There's a table being cleaned now, right this way."

She seated them at the table then disappeared into the kitchen. A moment later Alli appeared and grabbed Ebony in a bear hug. "Oh gods, Ebony, I can never thank you enough for rescuing me from that awful man. This is so amazing."

"You're happy?"

"That and so much more."

"Then I'm happy. Now put me down and hug Kar. I have somewhere else to be." Grinning, Ebony stepped out of Alli's arms and patted Kar on the shoulder. "Surprise. Talk to each other, ladies." With that she walked away.

Kar had risen slowly to her feet and now she and Alli stood silently gazing at each other shyly. "Oh for pity's sake," said Silan, who was serving the next table. She put her hand on Alli's back and gently guided her into Kar's arms.

Alli was instantly hugged tightly, listening to Kar whisper her name over and over. "Oh gods, Kar, I've missed you so much."

"Me too, sweetheart. I've been completely lost without you."

"Sit down, girls," grinned Silan. She guided them into the chairs then set a pot of tea on the table. Alli started to rise, but Silan stopped her. "We've got this, Alli. You and your lady talk to each other."

"Okay, thanks, Silan." The girl patted her shoulder and sped away. Alli sighed and gazed shyly at Kar. "Kar, what happened was all my fault, and I know that."

"No, Alli, it was me who pulled away, I ..."

"I know what you did, and I know why you did it. You tried to make it easier for me to move on. Kar, I learned something truly important in all this. Do you think we could start over?"

"I'd rather pick up where we left off."

"Oh so would I. Kar, I've missed you more than you can imagine."

"Me too, honey. How did we get so messed up?"

"We had help."

"Excuse me?"

"We both had relationships before that went sour, and we brought some of those old fears into this one, old habits too. I wanted to learn what that master chef could teach me, and I got so busy at first that it took me days to message you."

"And I misread that as you wanting to move on, so I didn't respond, tried to let you go gracefully. That didn't work so well, I've been lost without you. So, tell me how you ended up here?"

"I was on leave and looking for you. Ebony found me, listened to my sad story, and promised to fix it for me. This wonderful place is all her doing. I'll love her forever for this."

"She did all this for you?"

"For us, Kar. Yes, she wanted to help me get back on the Reacher, but I know darn well she wanted me here for you too. Kar, we both know she could have leaned on the chef in the mess and got me back there, but she wanted something more for me, for us, and for the rest."

"The rest?"

"The folks who're working here with me. A couple of the folks in the kitchen plus the girls out here. She knows them, or rather she found them, people like herself, folks with a lot of energy and no way to use it. She found them, trained them, and set this up. She mainly did this for us, but she did it for them too."

"Miriam told me Ebony confessed she wants to help all the young grounders find a place here. This gave her the chance to do some of that."

"Well, I for one, applaud her efforts, and like you said, I'll love her forever for bringing you back to me."

"Kar, as much as I hate to do this ..."

"You have to get back to work?"

"I do. Come for me at closing time?"

"Count on it, pretty woman. Off you go to the kitchen now, and I have to go report."

* * * * *

As Ebony left the café, her comm pinged. "Ensign Ebony Graves to the bridge briefing room."

Wide-eyed, she replied. "On my way." She was puffing when she arrived as she'd run most of the way.

"Come in, Ebony, have a seat," smiled Amanda.

Ebony swallowed hard. She knew who these people were but had no idea what they wanted. "Thank you, Vice-Admiral."

Jeannie chuckled as she leaned forward to brace her elbows on the table. "Relax, girl, you're not in any trouble. Quite the contrary, we asked you here to offer you a new position."

"Admiral?"

"Captain Moore tells me it was you who conceived of, then manifested the Simple Pleasures café. Tell me how that came about."

"Ah, ..."

"Remember, I'm SUVI. I'll know if you try to hold out on me. No excess modesty now, Ebony. This is important, tell me all of it."

"Yes, ma'am. A friend of mine had transferred to the Orca but was unhappy there. Yet another friend was unhappy without her here. I found Alli in the mess trying to get her old job back, but it was a bust. I had to escort her out of the crew mess as she was no longer a crew member.

"On our way out it hit me, she really wasn't truly happy here either. The thing is, Alli is a genius in the kitchen, but always getting held back by the head chefs, or the constraints of the job. She needed a way to be free to explore what she can do.

"The other person needed to have her back on the Reacher, so I hatched a plan. If it worked out, I could bring Alli home, reunite the lovers, and find better jobs for a few more unhappy folk as well. I went to Miriam Holbrooke with the idea, and she loved it.

"She called in Social Engagement, Sandy found us a space, I went to Antha for help to locate the people Alli would need to help her, found some old VR training programs to give them a boost to their skills, then was called out to fly EX4.

"Miriam took over and ran with it. End result, happy people all around and I get my favorite desserts back. It's all good."

Jeannie was smiling with delight. "Yes it is, girl, it is indeed all good. I'm curious, how was Antha able to help you?"

"I learned she's been the acting ship's counselor for some time. I told her what I needed for people and asked her to send any likely clients she might have to me or to Miriam. Next day they all showed up, unhappy at their jobs, or wishing they could get a job, something useful to do. They loved the idea and were really enthusiastic."

Jeannie leaned back and smiled. "Ebony, I am seriously impressed. I have a job for you if you're willing."

Wide eyed, Ebony met her gaze. "May I ask what it is, Admiral?"

"I really like the idea you had of using VR for preliminary training. I'd like to instill the practice throughout the fleet. The problem is, all the VR we have was developed on Old Earth. Much of it is no longer relevant to the way we live now, or to what we'll need in the future.

"For example, when we discovered the Orca, we suddenly needed more engineers, Moira had to train several people from scratch. VR could have seriously sped up that process."

"You want me to produce VR training modules for every department?"

"Yes, as well as specialized training, like you did for yourself. Ebony, you don't have to do it all alone, find the people who can help you, make the modules for you, then make it easy for them to succeed, just like you did with Simple Pleasures."

"Wow, Commander White was right."

"Explain."

"He warned me to never let you know my dreams unless I was ready to see them come true. Admiral, if you're serious, I'll give this my best shot."

"I am serious, Ebony. When I first came aboard the Reacher, Captain Baris made me an ensign and I reported directly to him. I was supposed to have full access to the ship.

"However, the rank of ensign wasn't enough, some crew members still didn't show me proper respect, and I had to exert my superior abilities. Captain Baris then promoted me to Sub-Commander, a rank that gained me more and better access, more respectful responses from the crew.

"So, I now promote you to Sub-Commander. You will be working for Vice-Admiral Drake, and you will be in charge of producing training VR modules for every department of the Reacher plus whatever the captains of the smaller ships might need. Eventually the Orca may have a few different ones for you to come up with.

"Also, you will be available to Security as pilot for EX4 as needed."

"I still get to fly?"

Jeannie chuckled at that. "Yes, you do. I've seen you fly; you'd make a fine SUVI with those reflexes. Go get a new uniform then report to Vice-Admiral Drake at her office. She'll get you started."

"Yes, ma'am." Ebony leapt to her feet and fled the room.

Rhonda chuckled. "Looks like you'll have a tiger by the tail, Amanda."

"She's going to tire me out just watching her go."

"Have you got a plan?" asked Jeannie.

"Oh heck no, not my job, it's her job. I'll get her started then sit back and watch her operate. She'll have my job in no time."

"So, does that mean you'll take over my job and I can go back to exploring?"

"Forget that, my super SUVI. If you go exploring, I go exploring. We'll hand the fleet over to Rhonda and Ebony, then we can retire ..."

"Oh no," said Rhonda. "Oh no you don't. You're not getting away with that. I'm not listening to any more of that kind of talk, I hear the bridge calling me." With that she rose and left the room, followed by Jeannie and Amanda's laughter.

* * * * *

Ebony arrived at Amanda's office in a fresh uniform with the Sub-Commander insignia on it. Amanda and Sandra Okomora were waiting for her. "Greetings, Sub-Commander Graves."

"Greetings, Ensign Okomora. Can we go back to being Ebony and Sandy? This new rank will take a bit of getting used to."

Sandra chuckled at that. "Works for me, Ebony."

"And within this office, ladies, I'm just Amanda. What happens next with this project is all you, Ebony. My task here is to make that as easy as possible for you, that's why Sandy's here."

"And mine as well," said Sandra. "I'll be your main connection to Social Engagement. Where do you want to start?"

Ebony took the chair Amanda indicated. "I guess I'll need someplace to work first, you know, something a bit bigger than an office."

"You'll need an office too," said Amanda. "I pulled a few strings and Jake agreed to give you the one next to mine."

Ebony's eyes opened wide at that. "He moved his office for me?"

"He did. I told him what you're doing, and he loved the idea. He agreed to move so we could work closely but asked that you start with Security."

She laughed with delight. "Easy as pie, I've already got those. I used them to prepare for the training, that's how I made it through so fast. We can use them as a guide to make a couple of new ones, to get a feel for how it's done."

"Sounds good," smiled Sandra. "What sort of space are we looking for to make the magic in?"

"It doesn't need to be too big, maybe twice the size of Simple Pleasures. Is that possible?"

"Shouldn't be a problem, I'll go see what I can find."

"And I'll go talk to Antha."

Amanda chuckled at that. "Looking for more people at loose ends?"

"Yeah. The way we lived in the caverns, and still do on the ships to an extent, doesn't leave a lot of options for people who are more artistic than military minded. For Alli, for instance, there was work in the mess, but it's organized in military fashion. No way for her to stretch herself, see what she could do.

"I'm betting there's lots more folks who would like a shot at some of this."

Sandra smiled wistfully at that. "Ebony, we've been trying and trying to find ways to get more people involved with the theatre groups. It never occurred to any of us to consult Antha about this. This project could go a long way to getting an acting troupe on the go."

* * * * *

Ebony entered Antha's office and was greeted warmly. "Ebony, welcome. Is that a Sub-Commander's insignia I see on your uniform?"

"Yep, I got a new job."

"Wonderful, dear friend. Share the joy, what are you up to now?"

"The admiral wants me to create training VR programs for every department on the ship, and more. She gave me the promotion."

"And you came to me looking for more people?"

"You know I did," chuckled Ebony. "Antha, those folks you sent to Alli are pure magic. They're as excited about the café as she is."

"I know, I was there with Linsey and Eighteen yesterday. My waistline may never recover. So, what sort of people are we looking for this time?"

"I need a digital genius, a computer artist, somebody who spends their time creating imaginary worlds in VR so they don't have to live in this one."

"What's the plan for this person?"

"I get my VR training modules created, the creator learns they have something of great value to contribute to the real world, a reason to crawl out of the shell. I have no idea if it'll work, but it's worth a shot."

"Ebony, you should be in my job, you're the one with the real training."

"Training is one thing, Antha, but you're a natural, you have exceptional instincts for this work. I don't. I want to help people, yes, but I don't have your knack for it. I can use that training to help me find the people I need and maybe help them find their way, but you're the one for this job.

"So, have you got anybody for me?"

"I do, a rather unique person, painfully shy, brilliant with the digital world, but almost non-functional in reality. There's another issue as well."

"Oh?"

"Edran is gender fluid."

"Edran, Edran, I know that name. Is Edran from the Caverns?"

"Yes, a young child traumatized by that experience, extremely withdrawn, terrified that, with nothing of great value to offer, expulsion or exile looms daily. No amount of reassurance seems to help."

"Send Edran to my office, they sound perfect."

"The mother will accompany them, elsewise they won't show up. She constantly reads to Edran to keep them focused when out of quarters."

"Not a problem, Antha. Send them along as soon as you can. I've just had a great idea."

Chapter #13

Decisions

Two weeks later, Rhonda was waiting as Amanda and Captain Grill of the Att't arrived in the transportation area. "Captain Grill, welcome to the Reacher, I'm Captain Rhonda Moore, and this is my first officer, Commander Jake White."

"Thank you, Captain Moore. I'm honored to be permitted to visit your ship."

"Perhaps, once the Admiral and Vice-Admiral have completed your meeting, you'd like a tour of the Reacher."

"It would be a great pleasure, Captain."

"Then I leave you to it."

Amanda smiled and gently touched Captain Grill's arm. "Right this way, Captain Grill. The admiral is in her office."

She led off and he followed closely. They found Jeannie deep in conversation with Moira Duncan, Chief Engineer for the fleet. Jeannie looked up and smiled. "Welcome, Captain Grill, please be seated. We were just discussing your ship."

"Oh?"

"Yes, but I fear the news isn't good."

"So, Commander Duncan, you and your team confirm the findings of my own engineers?"

"Aye, Captain. The damage to your ship was extensive on a structural level. She'll still fly, and she's capable of sustaining life, but I wouldn't risk an interstellar jump in her."

Grill fairly melted into the chair, his hand stroking his leathery face. "As I feared, but that no longer matters. Too few of us survived to fly her, and the mission is irrelevant now as there's no way to return the information to the home world.

"I requested this meeting today, Admiral, to ask to join your fleet. Alas, it seems that is no longer possible. Commander Duncan, is there nothing at all to be done?"

"Aye, in time you could rebuild and restructure, but, with your small crew it would take years."

"So, we're finished then. The great adventure of the Maccay into the unknown grinds to a halt."

"May I ask what the original mission was, Captain Grill?" asked Amanda.

"To learn new things, see what wonders were out beyond our scope, beyond our system. Was there anything else out there? Any other forms of life? What other wonders were there to be discovered? We're a curious people, we Maccay, Vice-Admiral, we always want to learn new things."

Amanda smiled and patted his arm then turned to Jeannie. "Admiral?"

"Yes, Mandy, I do agree, but we have to put this before the captains." Seeing Captain Grill's puzzled look, she smiled. "Moira, is the Captain's ship worth salvaging?"

"No, Admiral, at least not for us, and they don't have the numbers to fly her anyway."

Jeannie turned back to Grill. "Captain, as things stand now, you have two options. One, remain here and soldier on; two, join our fleet as you requested, but without your ship."

"You mean be absorbed into the crews of the fleet; my few remaining people scattered through the various ships?"

"Yes, and no. Captain, the Reacher has roughly a thousand souls aboard who are passengers, not crew. They're members of a failed human colony, plus the families of the crew. Reacher is the home ship; Orca is the guardian.

"Your people would be considered passengers but would be free to apply for crew positions just as anyone else. We may yet build more small ships, explorers, and the like. Another ship would need crew. Something to think about, for certain."

"You would do that? You'd take us in?"

"I'll have to consult with the other captains, especially Captain Moore and her senior staff, but I doubt there would be a problem. There's also yet another possibility that occurs to me.

"In the next system is a species who have fallen back into a more primitive lifestyle, yet they have a viable ship. However, it needs repairs and they have only one man who understands the ship and its functions."

"The one you spoke of, he who originally defeated the Wrax."

"Ka'Ron, yes."

Captain Grill sat up straighter. "Admiral, I came here fearing the worst news, and that came. However, you present me with other possibilities. I have much to think about, much to take back to my people. Just as you must consult your people, so must I, for I cannot make these decisions without their input."

"Understood, Captain. I'll see if I can get someone to give you a tour of the Reacher so you can relate that back to your people."

"Captain Moore has already graciously offered to do just that, Admiral. That tour has just taken on far greater importance than my mere curiosity."

"Then I'll leave you to it. Mandy, put the captain and Rhonda together, then call the captains in for a conference."

The meeting was called, and Jake, as first officer of the Reacher, conducted the captain's tour.

* * * * *

Jeannie put the idea of absorbing the Maccay into their combined peoples before the captains. Nobody had any real objections, but most were hesitant to speak. Finally, Rhonda broke the silence.

"Okay, let's have a look at this. These folks have a ship that's not really worth repairing, they've lost over half their crew, and if we take them in, I'll end up with the lot of them as passengers. Am I right?"

"Rhonda?"

"Please, Admiral, I'm not objecting in any way here, I'm not. I'm just trying to look at this from a different angle. They're a pacifist species, refused to even arm their ship for defense."

"Yes, but where are you going with this?"

"Admiral, as such they won't serve as crew on Orca, maybe on one of the small ships, but the real issue here will be to find them ways to fit in, things to do to keep them sane. They're curious I'm told. Curiosity and boredom can mean a world of trouble.

"We need to find a way to help them that will give them things to occupy themselves ..."

"Is easy," said Sessas. All eyes turned to her. At Jeannie's nod she went on. "Grill have small crew, bad ship. Ka'Ron have good ship, no trained crew, want to fix ship, fly with fleet."

Jeannie chuckled at that and sat back in her chair. "Sessas, are you suggesting we put Ka'Ron and Grill together, see if they can help each other?"

"Yes. Grill help Ka'Ron, Ka'Ron help Grill. All good."

"What do you think, people? Personally, I think Sessas' idea has merit."

"So do I," agreed Sheila, "and it solves a lot of problems. It gives Ka'Ron the help he needs, and it gives Grill's people a viable ship, jobs to occupy their minds. I'll support that."

"Works for me," agreed Rhonda. "Please don't misunderstand, I have no objections to having them on the Reacher, but I can see possible issues. This idea looks better from here."

There was a round of agreement from the others and Captain Grill was brought back in to hear the proposed idea. He sat quietly and listened, nodding from time to time. When Jeannie finished outlining the idea he agreed, the idea had possibilities.

"I like it, Admiral," he said at last. "This would give my people productive things to do, a ship to fly and explore from, and more. If not, then we simply sit here and await our eventual death. We set out to explore the universe, this will allow us to continue that mission, give those of us who survived a reason to continue living."

* * * * *

While Jeannie held her top level meeting, Ebony sat quietly in her office, waiting. It had taken the full two weeks to finally convince Edran to come for the interview. During that two weeks she'd been playing a series of new games in VR, games designed and built by Edran.

Antha had convinced the mother to share them with Ebony. Edran was definitely the right one for the job, now it was up to Ebony to convince the young genius to do it. This was not going to be easy. She almost jumped as a soft knock came at the door. "Come in."

A woman with a careworn face entered, holding a reading tablet in one hand, and gently tugging a rather androgynous looking teenager with the other. "Welcome, folks. Have a seat."

They sat and the teen pulled their elbows tight to their body and stared at their hands in their lap. "Hey, Edran, remember me? I was in the caverns too." A nod was the only response she got.

The mother spoke next. "Antha said you have a job for Edran? I'm not sure ..."

"Forgive me," smiled Ebony, "but I think Edran's the one for the job all right." She pushed the small info block across her desk towards Edran. "These three games were pretty cool, but it was number three that gave me fits. Those worm things jumping out of the flying meteors scared the lights out of me the first few times."

That brought a nervous giggle from Edran. "Edran, as much fun as the games were, it was the world building that I liked. Your imagination is even wilder than mine, and that's saying a lot. So, here's the deal.

"My job is to make training VR programs for every department on the ship, all the ships, every possible thing. No, actually, that's your job; my job is to help you make that happen. What do you say, want to give it a try?"

"Stupid. Any fool can do that."

"Edran!"

"No, no, Edran's right, if you do it the old way. The thing is, both Edran and I know something nobody else knows, don't we, Edran?"

There was a long silent pause. "What's that?"

Ebony grinned with delight. This was going to work. "Edran, we both survived the caverns, and we came out smarter than most everybody else. Why? Because we spent so much time in VR. Yes, we played games, but we learned a ton of stuff too, right? The thing we both know is, people learn more things a lot faster through play."

"Yeah, I guess."

"You know it, my friend. That's why I want you on this job. Like you say, anybody can make a training VR, but can they make a VR game that trains someone for a specific task? In truth I'm not really sure it can be done."

That brought a full response. "Oh yes it can, if you can get the right equipment."

"You sure?"

"I can do it ..." Edran stopped, the enthusiasm suddenly falling away into fear and the gaze returned to their hands."

Ebony pretended not to notice. "Equipment, eh? Hmmm. Well, I've got a studio all set up in the grand mall area, right near Simple Pleasures Cafe. Come check it out for me and I'll get Alli to sneak us a few treats. How about it, check it out and let me know if I've got the right equipment?"

"I could do that, I guess."

"Awesome, let's go. I want to plug in that game with the meteors into the big equipment, see what it looks like with some real power running it."

"It'll scare you," came the soft voice as Edran rose to follow her out of the office. Ebony chuckled as she led them to her new studio. She chatted easily to Edran about the joys of hiding from life in the caverns by spending endless hours in VR.

By the time they arrived they were discussing various games they'd played. Edran's mother just watched in amazement as Ebony didn't try to pull her child out of the fantasy world, but went in with Edran, went with them to a place where they felt safe.

One look at the computer setup in the corner of the studio and Edran was hooked. Ebony was in awe as Edran used both keyboard and voice commands to create a completely new world right before her eyes. She left them and went next door to talk to Alli.

Ebony returned with three pieces of cake. "What do you think, Edran, will this setup do what it needs to do?"

"Oh yeah, this rocks. Here you go, a new world. It's pretty basic now but give me a few days and I can make it sing. This is amazing, so fast, … sorry."

Ebony was grinning. "So, you like my toys, do you? Want to do a test case?"

"Test case?"

"It has to be more than a game, Edran. The game has to teach a certain skill. Can you do it?"

"With this equipment? Easy."

"Okay, hot shot, here's a video of a woman baking a cake. And here's the actual cake. Taste it."

One taste and Edran devoured the cake. "That was great."

"Okay, so the video I gave you shows exactly how it's done. Make me the VR and I'll get someone to test it. Now, here's the dangerous part. Once the volunteer has played the game then baked the cake, you and I are going to watch the real chef taste it. If she says it's a go, then we put that VR on the training list. If not, we blew it and have to try again. You up for the challenge?"

"Sure, no problem."

"How much time do you need?"

"Three days maybe."

"Okay, Edran. You're smarter than most folks, so you already know what's going to happen here, right?"

"This is an easy one for a start, then they get harder and harder, right?"

"Right. Remember, this game is to train a chef, not a warrior. The next one might be security, or pilot training, or god knows what. It's a game where we see what level we can reach, and we can help a lot of folks while we do it."

This time Edran looked up and made full eye contact. "How can I make a VR for flying a ship? I'm not a pilot? What about engineering or ...?"

"That's where I do my job, my friend. I'll make the videos, record interviews, etc. and bring them to you, you use them to help you build the games. We'll get actors to help if we need them. This is a team effort, you and me together, two kids from the caverns. What do you say, will you help me show all these folks that we're not useless, show them they need us if they want to survive?"

Suddenly Edran was in Ebony's arms, tears running freely as great sobs shook their body. Finally, as the storm of emotion passed, Edran responded. "Yes, let's do this. Can I start on that test case now?"

Ebony gave Edran another gentle squeeze then relaxed her arms. "Okay, but first, have another piece of the cake, you know, just so you're sure what it is we're trying to create, right?" Edran giggled and accepted the plate. They practically inhaled the cake then set to work, watching a few moments of the video then working at the computer.

Smiling, Ebony turned to the mother. "Good thing you brought a reading tablet, looks like you'll be here a while."

"That's okay. Sub-Commander Graves, I can't thank you enough for this, I don't know what to say."

"Look, I believe I've got Edran on board, now it's your turn."

"Excuse me? My turn?"

"For the job offer."

"Job offer? I don't understand."

"We can't do all this alone, Edran and I, we just can't. You've been reading to them all their life, keeping them focused, etc. There will be tons of material that will need to be read aloud as we work our way through all this. Edran is accustomed to listening to your voice for instruction, for direction, and you've got years of experience reading aloud. That's a mighty skill in its own right. Will you help us, be our reader?

"It's going to take years if we can ever get it all done. This is a full-time job; will you take it on?"

The woman's eyes were shining as she nodded her head. "How is it supposed to work? When do I start?"

"I'll get a reading booth set up for you in here. Edran will be able to see you from there, but you'll be in a sound-proof room. I'm sure there'll be lots of times when you'll have to come out and read directly to Edran, and I want them to be comfortable with that situation. Thank you for taking this on for us."

"Thank you for all you've done here, Sub-Commander."

"Ebony. Just Ebony is fine."

"Thank you, Ebony. I'm Elaine, and I owe you more than you know."

"Do not, Elaine. We're all refugees from the caverns. We were rescued, but we're pretty much on our own trying to find how we can fit in, be useful, valuable to the greater society. I got lucky, so I plan to use my new position to help as many other refugees as I can, refugees and sky-riders alike. Not everybody is working crew, and not all working crew should be."

* * * * *

One week later there were nervous people in the studio. Edran had finished the game in three days then it had been handed over to Jake

White, the first officer. It was late, and Simple Pleasures had been closed for hours, but two of the tables were full. Alli, Kar, Jeannie, Amanda, Rhonda, Carla, and SUVI 20, sat chatting easily while they waited. Jake was busy in the kitchen.

Ebony, Elaine, and Edran paced about nervously in the studio next door while Jake baked the cake. Eventually he emerged from the kitchen carrying the cake and set it on the table in front of Alli. She looked it over carefully, trying to frown, but failing. "Looks perfect, Commander," she smiled. "Now for the taste test."

Everyone held their breath as she cut a slice and looked it over, then delicately took a taste, holding it in her mouth, savoring the flavor. Everyone began to cheer as the grin of delight spread over her face. "Perfect. Absolutely perfect. Folks, you have to taste this."

Alli dished out the cake and Jake went next door to fetch Ebony and friends. Edran and Elaine sat with Ebony while the cake was demolished. When it was gone, Jake grinned with delight and brought out another one from the kitchen. That was soon shared around too.

Jeannie laid her fork on the empty plate and sighed with contentment. "Ebony, I confess I had my doubts about this experiment of yours, but you've done it."

"I agree," chimed in Twenty. "In three days you've taken Jake from completely inept in the kitchen to a professional baker of wonder cake. You're amazing."

Ebony beamed with pleasure. "Actually, it wasn't me, it was Edran. I filmed Alli baking the cake, then Edran built the game to teach how it's done. This was Edran's work all the way."

The slight teenager sat gazing at their hands, but beaming with delight at the praise. "Edran, you came from the caverns too, didn't you?" said Jeannie. "I remember seeing you there. This is amazing work, my young friend. What you create over the next few years will be invaluable to the people for generations to come."

"If you don't scare them to death first," grumbled Jake. "I swear, if that damned oven had exploded on me one more time, I was going to use Twenty's war hammer on it." Edran giggled at that.

"Exploding oven, Jake?" asked Jeannie.

"Yep. Every time I got something wrong, even by the slightest amount, the oven would explode on me, scared the crap out of me the first few times. I will admit, I've gained a new respect for the magic Alli whips up every day."

"So, will you bake another one when we get home?" asked Carla. There was more laughter as he groaned in protest.

Jeannie smiled at Ebony. "Looks like you're on the right track, Ebony. Well done. Now that you young geniuses know your method works, what are you going to tackle next?"

"My deal with Jake says we have to work on Security next."

"Actually, I'd like to overrule that," said Rhonda. "Engineering has installed new sensors, weapons, and more on my ship in the past few months. We have trained people, but too few of them. If anything happens, anything at all, an untrained crewman, or someone unfamiliar with the equipment's true abilities, could suddenly be in a position they don't feel competent to handle. If possible, I'd like you to start with the bridge crew."

"Ah, well, I ..."

"It's your decision, Ebony," said Jeannie. "This is your baby, and you have the whole fleet to think about, but the decision is yours to make."

Ebony sighed then nodded. "Captain Moore is right. Reacher is the mother ship, the home ship. Orca's training their own crew, so we do need to start with Reacher, but the bridge is a big jump from where we are now."

"No it isn't," grinned Jake. "I'll take a bridge post any day over the kitchen. I don't know how you do it, Alli."

"We can do it," came a quiet voice.

Ebony winked at Amanda. "You sure, Edran? This is a big jump."

"We can do it, Ebony. Time for us to level up."

Ebony's grin broadened. "All right, Captain. First thing tomorrow I'll show up on the bridge with the camera. You can show me which station to start with and the order in which you want them done.

"Edran, we'll meet first so you can give me a list of what you'll need."

"Lots of camera angles of the bridge for a base, then tons more from the workstation."

"Okay, I can probably get a bunch of that from old security feeds. Go home and put some thought into how you're going to torture the bridge crew." Edran giggled at that.

* * * * *

As the party broke up, Rhonda was the last to leave, staying back to speak with Ebony for a moment about the bridge. She was barely away from Simple Pleasures on her way back to her quarters when she met Maxi coming the other way. "Captain Moore?"

"Hello, Maxi."

"What are you doing here? Simple Pleasures has been closed for hours."

"Actually, it wasn't, there was a special event going on tonight."

"Ebony's test case," enthused Maxi. "Did it work?"

"Like a charm," chuckled Rhonda. "Our first officer baked a perfect cake. The only thing he'd ever cooked in his life was raw meat over an open fire when he was stranded on Planet Stormy. He was the perfect choice for the test."

"Wow, and it worked. This is so great."

"Okay, Maxi, my instincts are working overtime here, tell me what's going on."

A naughty grin played at Maxi's lips, and her blue eyes were flashing as she replied. "Sure, but only if you walk me home."

Rhonda felt her cheeks redden and sighed. "You know it's against regulations to make the captain blush in public."

"Oh dear, my bad, sorry."

"You're not one bit sorry, woman," chuckled Rhonda. "Maxi, how have you managed to survive, being so painfully shy and all?"

Maxi's sweet laughter brought a grin of delight to Rhonda, and she knew she'd do anything to make the girl laugh. "Were you one of the colonists?"

"No, Captain, I was born on a ship, just like you were, the old Wanderer. We've never encountered each other before as I was working in stores, night shift, for the first few years of my less than brilliant career."

She linked her arm through Rhonda's then continued. "I was sulking to Antha about it one day and she sent me to Ebony. Ebony told me about the cafe getting set up, gave me some old training VRs that she had, and I ended up in my dream job."

"Serving in a café was your dream job?"

"Oh hell no, it had never crossed my mind. I just wanted a job where I could be with other people all day, stay on my feet, move around, instead of being chained to a desk. Simple Pleasures is great, I get to talk with lots of different people, I'm always on the go, and I bring them things that make them smile. The job's perfect for me."

"Wow. I have to say, that bright smile of yours is a real highlight of my trips to Simple Pleasures."

"Hey, now who's making who blush?"

"Sorry."

"You're not either. You did that to get me back."

"Busted. So, back to what's going on here."

"I'm flirting with you, Captain. I've been trying to catch your attention since the first time you walked into Simple Pleasures."

"Dammit, Maxi," blushed Rhonda. She was rewarded with that sweet laugh once again. "Save some of that naughtiness and tell me what you meant when you were so enthused about the VR experiment."

"Okay, I'll talk. It's Ebony, and her plan to help as many people as she can to find their place, their happy place. We're all trapped here on the ship, and we have to find where we fit in, how we can be useful to society and enjoy doing it.

"Ebony trained herself to be a psychologist like her mother but wanted to be a fighter pilot too. She got lucky, then even luckier. The admiral gave her the perfect job to do both. Captain, if all Ebony wanted to do was help Alli get back to Reacher she could have talked to the chef and got Alli her old job back.

"She wanted something more for her friend and came up with the cafe. Through that project she could help Alli, and a few more folks as well. Now, with this new job, she'll be able to help dozens of people. Not the super-hot shots like you and the main crew, but the lost, lonely, and unhappy of us, the unknowns, the ultra-shy like me, and more."

"Yes, I saw that in action tonight," mused Rhonda. "The person she has working on this is one of those people, isn't she?"

"They, Captain. Edran is three or more people all in the same body, and yes, they are genius. I can hardly wait to see who else Ebony pulls out of the woodwork. It's just so hard for some folks. On a planet with millions of people there must have been thousands of ways to shine, to make a difference."

"But on a ship, even one as big as the Reacher, not so much. I get that, Maxi. I do. Is there any way I can help?"

"Captain?"

"Rhonda. Rhonda is fine when we're alone."

"Does this mean we'll get more alone time together?"

"Dammit, Maxi, there you go again," sighed Rhonda, her cheeks coloring again to the sound of that silvery laugh she was learning to love.

"Is that a yes?"

"Okay, it's a yes, if you want that."

"I sure do. Tomorrow's my day off, and there's a new play opening at the theatre on the mall. Any chances for a date?"

"These your quarters?" asked Rhonda, as Maxi stopped walking.

"Yes."

"What time should I come for you?"

"Seven. Rhonda?"

"Yes?" Rhonda was keenly aware of Maxi stepping close, the touch of her sweet breath, the depth of those dazzling blue eyes.

"You walked the girl home, you should at least get a goodnight kiss, right?"

With a blush on her cheeks Rhonda pulled her close. "Gods you're naughty."

Maxi slid her arms around Rhonda's neck and let her eyes flutter closed as she leaned in for a kiss. "You like it."

Chapter #14

Incoming

It had been a month since the VR test and Jake was still getting teased about baking a cake for his wives. He just grinned every time. This day he was on the bridge of the Reacher for another VR test, a far more serious test. The captain, admiral, vice-admiral, and Ebony were also there.

Today there was a new man on the sensors. This man was from the caverns, had always worked in Hydroponics, and was in his sixties. He'd volunteered to test the VR to train a sensor officer. Commander Ortega was watching over his shoulder carefully. "You're doing great. Tell me what you see."

"I see the debris field, the star, planets and satellites, EX2, Retriever, the Att't, and the Orca, but I'm not sure what this is over here, out beyond the eighth planet."

Anita was leaning over closer, peering at the screen. "I can't see anything, show me."

"Right here, ma'am, it's small, only a flicker, but ... there."

"Yes, I saw that. Damn, you're good."

"What is it, Anita?"

"Unknown, Admiral, but ... there it is again. It seems to be moving with a purpose."

"A purpose?"

"It seems to want to stay hidden."

"Comms, get me the Orca."

"Reacher calling Orca."

"Orca here, Sheila Singh commanding."

"I have the admiral for you, Captain Singh. One moment. Go ahead, Admiral."

"Sheila, I'm aboard the Reacher. Our sensors have picked up something unnatural out beyond the eighth planet."

"We'll take a look, Admiral. Orca out." The Orca's shields went up and she practically vanished from the sensors.

Jeannie turned to Ebony and gave her a nod of approval. "Looks like you've got another winner here, Ebony." She just beamed her pleasure at the admiral's praise.

Anita turned from the sensors. "Captain Moore, I'd like to have every member of the bridge crew trained on this VR. Sub-Commander Graves, how soon can you get me a VR for every station of the bridge?"

"It's already in the works, but each one takes time. I can't thank you enough for all your help getting them set up."

Seeing Jeannie's raised eyebrow, Anita grinned. "I've been playing teacher for days, Admiral. Ebony has been filming me from morning until night while I work every station with its current officer, both of us carefully explaining each and every movement, every visual, every instrument, etc. I confess, before we gave this first one to Dave here, I tested it myself. It took me three tries to get through it."

Jeannie laughed at that. "Well done, Ebony. I had a sense this would be valuable, but I may have underestimated its possibilities."

At that point the Comms Officer spoke up. "I have the Orca for you, Admiral. Go ahead."

Jeannie stepped in front of the screen. "Sheila, did you find the object?"

"Yes and no, Admiral. Yes, we've picked it up on sensors, but as soon as we do it evades. Whatever this is, it does not want to be found. It's also trying to scan us, but our shields keep fooling it up."

"Have you tried hailing it?"

"No response and we've used every language in the database Linsey gave us."

"Does it pose a threat?"

"Unknown at this time, Admiral. We do know it's not big enough to be a ship, more likely a probe of some sort. My concern is what kind of a probe, and who sent it? What do you want to do here?"

"Keep an eye on it, learn what you can about it, and above all, be careful, Sheila. We know cloaking technology exists because we have it."

"Understood, Admiral. May I ask, how did Reacher spot this thing anyway?"

"Ebony's new training VR, Sheila. We found a man in Hydroponics to test it then today we put him on our sensors. He's the one who picked it up."

"Seriously? I want a copy of that training VR as soon as possible, and anything more she can dream up."

Jeannie beckoned Ebony forward and nodded. "I'll have a copy sent to you immediately, Captain Singh."

"Thank you, Ebony, and thank you for giving Ernel a copy of the cake VR."

Ebony laughed with delight. "You're welcome, Captain. I'll go back to my office now and transmit the VR for you."

As Ebony walked away, Jeannie turned to Rhonda. "Shields are up, and Reacher is on alert status, Admiral."

"Efficient as usual, Rhonda," grinned Jeannie.

"As I've said before, Admiral, I enjoy a bit of excitement, but I'm a cautious woman. We'll stay on alert until we're sure that thing poses no threat."

"Shall I recall the small ships?" asked Amanda.

"Yes, bring them back, Mandy. I want a conference with Eighteen and Thirteen. This object is making me a bit uneasy."

Amanda was on the comms as Jeannie walked away. The man at sensors stepped away to speak to Anita. "Commander, shall I return to Hydroponics now?"

"Stay right where you are, Mister. I want you on those damned sensors until we're sure that this thing is alone and that it poses no threat."

"Aye, Commander. Returning to sensors," he replied with a huge grin. Rhonda just shook her head and chuckled.

* * * * *

On the bridge of the Orca, there was a tense excitement, but the calm professional demeanor of the Captain and First and Second Officers kept things tightly controlled. "Sensors?"

"Recalibrating, Captain. Yes, I've got a clearer picture of this thing now."

"On screen." The big forward screen lit up with a small faceted globe flashing in the rays of the distant sun. It instantly spun to face some sort of instrument at them then it darted away, attempting to hide behind the planet. Orca moved with it, and it returned to the screen.

"Is it targeting us?"

"I don't believe so, Captain, but it is trying to scan us," replied the woman on sensors. "It doesn't want us to see it, but it wants to see us."

"Can you estimate its size?"

"The object is roughly the size of one of our small fighter ships, Captain."

"So, in theory, it could pose a threat."

Brandon Hoffman agreed. "It could. I wonder what it would do if we launched a fighter, gave it more than one thing to observe."

"It could also be a ship with a full crew aboard," said Emmet Jones, the Second Officer. "The Earalith were a species of small stature, but they built a vast empire."

Sheila chuckled at that. "Why Emmet, since when did you indulge in such wild speculation?"

He retained his poker face, but the twinkle in his eye gave it away as he replied. "Just trying to present you with all the possibilities, Captain."

That bit of gentle banter brought a few smiles to the bridge crew and dispelled a lot of the tension. Finally the captain spoke again. "Sensors, is it broadcasting anything?"

"No, Captain."

"Is it transmitting anything to anywhere that you can detect?"

"Detecting no transmissions of any kind from the object, Captain. Wait, there might be something ..."

"Talk to me."

"Captain, there's a stream of some sort of impulses from the object, but they're being aimed into empty space. The nearest thing we can detect in that direction is the Andromeda Galaxy or perhaps a different arm of this one."

"Curious and curiouser," mused Sheila. "Comms, get the admiral for me."

"Aye, Captain. Orca calling Reacher."

"Sorenson here."

"The object seems to be about the size of a small Wrax fighter ship, Admiral," said Sheila. "It's sending out some sort of pulsing beam that is apparently aimed out into intergalactic space."

"Seriously? Is it making any threatening moves at all?"

"None, Admiral, but it is still using evasive maneuvers. What do you want to do here?"

"Keep your guard up, Sheila, but have your engineers see if they can learn anything more about it."

"Understood. Orca out.

"Dorind, can you tell me anything more about this object?"

"No, Captain. I'm sorry, but without better instruments I can learn nothing more unless we bring it into the hold where I can get my hands on it."

"I see."

* * * * *

While the bridge crew of Orca kept watch over the object, Jeannie met with SUVI 13 and SUVI 18. "Something is amiss, Five," said Eighteen, as they entered the admiral's office.

"We've discovered an object out by Planet 8. It's making no threat so far, but it is trying to hide from us. It is also sending out some sort of impulses into intergalactic space. Can you tell me anything at all about this object?"

Eighteen closed her eyes for a few moments then spoke, her eyes now open and glowing amber. "The object has been here a very long time. I don't believe it is harmful, in fact, I get the impression it should be useful to us."

"Really? Thirteen, if we pull this thing in, can you give me anything on the outcome?"

The lean hard man sat meditating quietly, neither woman made any move to disturb him. He sighed and allowed his eyes to return to their natural brown. "It's all quite unclear, Five, but it does appear we will be better off with it than without it. I see us using this thing like an advanced scout, to tell us if a system is inhabited or not. I believe we should find a way to capture it and put it to use."

"You mean convince it to help us."

"Eighteen?"

"I sense an AI mind at work here, Five. I've become somewhat familiar with them over the past few years."

Jeannie chuckled at that. "I bet you have. So, you both sense no threat here?"

"None, Five," replied Thirteen.

"Alright then, Eighteen, find your captain and crew; go out and see if you can help Sheila catch the elusive prey."

"On my way," grinned the small woman as she rose and left the office.

"Thirteen, did you ever hunt a Rellig on Elysium?"

He chuckled at that. "I tried. Caught one once, but it took both Twelve and I to bring it down, and then First Prime didn't like the meat anyway. So, you're thinking EX2 should be ready on standby?"

"Find your captain, Thirteen. Be ready if needed." He nodded and left the office. Jeannie returned to the bridge.

* * * * *

Back on the Orca the captain suddenly had an interesting thought. "Hmm, I wonder ..."

"Captain?"

"What do you think, Brandon, could those pulses be a code?"

"Possible, I guess. You're thinking about calling Captain da Silva?"

"Yes. Your opinion?"

"It can't hurt to get another pair of eyes with a different perspective to have a look at it."

"Comms, get me the admiral again."

"Sorenson here. What's up, Sheila?"

"This thing is still sending bursts or pulses out into space, Admiral. We can't make any sense out of it, but I wondered if ..."

"Linsey's already on her way. Sheila, I've consulted with SUVI 18 and SUVI 13, they sense no threat here, but believe we should investigate further."

"Understood."

Jeannie's image vanished from the forward screen and Sheila sighed. "Shall I lower the shields, Captain?" asked a voice.

"No. We stay on full alert until we're certain there's no threat. We'll wait a while yet."

"Aye, Captain."

A few moments later Friendship arrived, the shields were dropped, and it landed in the fighter bay of Orca. Linsey and Eighteen soon arrived on the bridge carrying their equipment. "Linsey, good to see you. With any luck you'll be able to make sense of this thing for me."

"I'll give it my best shot. Have you been recording those pulses for me?"

"Right here, Ma'am," smiled a young man as he passed her an info stick.

She plugged it into her machine, put on the headphones and listened for a few moments then took them off. "It's not a language, at least, not something I'd recognize as a language. I think we need to call in a special consultant on this one."

"Special consultant?" asked Sheila.

"My ship," grinned Linsey. "This object is a machine or an AI in a machine. Maybe Friendship can understand it. We'll go back and give it a shot."

Sheila nodded as Linsey left the bridge. "Sensors, don't lose track of that thing, whatever you do."

"Aye, Captain, tracking foreign object."

Linsey and Eighteen returned to Friendship. "That was quick, Captain."

"Yes it was, Ettelan, but we're not done yet. Ship, my friend, I have a request."

"Ship is at your command, Captain da Silva. How may I serve?"

"An object has been found in space. It is trying to evade us, and is transmitting short bursts of something, aimed out into empty space. I can't decipher the code or language or whatever this information is. I thought perhaps you might be able to make sense of it for me."

"This is interesting, but beyond my experience."

"All I ask is that you try, Friend Ship."

"There is great danger here, Captain da Silva."

"Oh? Explain?"

"If this is indeed transmitted data, it could contain codes that would damage or destroy Ship."

"Oh? I hadn't thought of that. Forgive me, my friend, we'll think of something else."

"No, Captain, Ship will take the risk, but I need to isolate and protect my core programming. This will take a few moments." Everyone sat quietly while the ship hummed softly. "Ship is prepared now. Insert information stick at station two."

Linsey stepped to the softly flashing light and inserted the stick. An hour later the flashing light stopped, and the stick was ejected. "Ship has decoded the information, Captain da Silva."

"So, what was it?" asked Linsey as she retrieved the info stick and returned it to her pocket.

"The object was recording the movements of the fleet and sending that information back to its creators. Ship expects that the object was brought to this system by the same methods that Reacher was. Ship would be able to discover much more if a direct link could be established."

"Thank you, ship. Would a direct link pose any threat to you?"

"None, Captain da Silva."

"Does this object or its creators pose any threat to the fleet?"

"None. The object is for observation only, and the creators are too far away, if they still exist at all."

"All right, good to know. I'll go inform the captain of the Orca now." With that Linsey left Friendship and returned to the bridge of the warship."

"Linsey, what's the good word?" asked Sheila.

"It's a probe from another galaxy, or far across on the other side of this one; brought here the same way we were. It's been watching us and sending the information back to its home, but I doubt if any of that information has reached there yet. Friendship says he can learn a lot more if we can get him a direct link to the probe. He also says there's no threat, the probe is an observer, a gatherer of information only."

"Good to know, stand down alert, lower shields. Sensors, keep a sharp eye on that thing, do not let it out of your sight. Comms, get me the admiral."

"Sorenson here. Tell me good things, people."

"It's a probe, Admiral," replied Linsey. "It's likely from another galaxy or the other side of this one; got here the same way we did, and is still following its programming, sending the information it gathers back home."

"Tell me, Linsey, how did you learn all this?"

She laughed with delight at Linsey's response. "I couldn't make sense of it, so I asked Friendship to take a shot at it. He says he can tell us a lot more if we can get him a direct link."

"Can that be done safely?"

"Ship says it can, but we'll have to catch the darn thing first."

"We'll make it happen then. I'll come over with F1 and lead the hunt. Sorenson out." As she left the bridge of the Reacher, she was back on the comms again. "Captains Morthel, Sessas, and Commander Hal White, get your ships ready and follow F1. We're going hunting for a Rellig."

"Hal here, Admiral. May I ask, what's a Rellig?"

"A thing that is extremely hard to catch," was her laughing reply. "We'll all meet aboard the Orca to coordinate the hunt."

* * * * *

Two days later they were back in the briefing room of the Orca. Suddenly Jeannie started to laugh. "It's not funny, Five," groused SUVI 13.

"This Rellig certainly is elusive," grinned Jeannie. "Thirteen, you know what the problem is here."

"We're working in three dimensions instead of two. That renders the problem nearly impossible to solve."

"Nearly?"

"Yes, Captain Morthel, nearly. There is a possible solution, and I'm sure Five has figured it out," sighed Thirteen. "That's why she's laughing at me."

Jeannie was still chuckling. "Come on, Thirteen, you know the answer."

He finally grinned. "I assume by Captain Moore's presence here today we're going to chase that elusive Rellig in between moons three and four with Orca above and Reacher below, thus cutting down the field. That takes us back to two dimensions instead of three."

"That's the plan. Will it work, do you think?"

"I'd say it's our best bet," he agreed.

"All right folks, here we go," said Jeanie. "Computer, display three dimensional scan of Planet Eight and her satellites." The hologram of the planetary system appeared above the long table. "Include ships in the area." The ships appeared.

"I want Orca here, just above these two moons, Rhonda, you come up under here, Sessas, you and Hal block this area here, leaving this passage open. Morthel and I will chase the prey into the trap then block the escape. Once we have it trapped, Linsey brings Friendship in beside F1 then tries to make contact.

"All right, let's go trap a Rellig."

* * * * *

It took longer than they expected. The elusive probe had observed the ships moving into position, recording their movements, then sending the information out into deep space. Once the trap was set, F1 and EX2 went on the hunt. The people on the other ships observing their movements were somewhat confused, as they appeared to be ignoring the prey.

Suddenly Sheila grinned. "I see what they're doing."

"Seriously?"

"Yes, Brandon. Look, it always shies away and hides when anyone gets close. It's acting like a young puppy who's lost and wants to make friends but is too fearful to come close. Somebody gets too close, and she shies away. They're patient, those SUVI hunters, but look, it's almost in the tra ... Gotcha. There's nowhere to run now, my elusive little friend."

The sounds of wild cheering could be heard on every ship as the small probe hung quietly in the trap. Realizing it was caught, it had powered down. They all watched their screens as Friendship moved past F1, almost scraping the sides together.

Information bursts flew from Friendship to the probe. No response. Friendship moved closer and tried again. Still no response. Linsey moved her ship closer still and tried again. This time there was a sudden response. Information passed between them at speeds far too fast for humans to follow.

At length it slowed to a trickle, then they heard Linsey's voice. "Reacher, requesting permission to land with my new friend."

"Is that safe to do, Linsey?"

"It is, Rhonda. Friendship has established rapport with the probe. Probe will comply with commands from this ship."

"Permission granted, Friendship. Landing bay opening."

"Rhonda, Jeannie here. Bring the others aboard, then transport Sheila over. Sorenson to Vice-Admiral Drake."

"Full top level meeting?"

"Yes."

"On it. Drake out."

* * * * *

"All requested personnel present, Admiral."

"Thank you, Mandy. Okay folks, we've caught the elusive probe. Linsey, report. What can you tell us about this shy creature?"

"Probe 373578 is an interesting story, Admiral, and she has given us greater insights into what happened to us and those others who ended up here.

"Probe 373578 was originally built and deployed to keep an eye out for the Wrax in their sector. Unfortunately, if you're spying on the

Wrax, you need to be stealthy, and Probie was built just for that task. She was keeping a close eye on a Wrax warship when it got jerked out of its reality and deposited here, along with the mechanical spy.

"She's been here ever since, spying on the Wrax ship and relaying information back to her home world. Admiral, that world is in another galaxy. It's doubtful the home world still exists, or has life on it. Also, there is no way for Probie to get home, the distance is too great.

"Friendship convinced her to share what information she has, and any tech we can gain without compromising her. He trusts us and she trusts him."

"You talk like they're actual people," said Hal.

"Are people, Hal," said Sessas, "just different. Sessas different, Morthel different, SUVI different, and Friendship different. All different, still people."

Hal grinned ruefully. "Yes, you're right, Captain Sessas. All people, different, but the same."

"Yes, different, but same. People."

"So you've given the probe a name, Linsey," smiled Jeannie.

"It was easier than trying to remember all the numbers."

"I see. So, continuing the line of discussion, do you see this probe as an individual capable of independent thought, of making reasoned decisions?"

"I do, Admiral. Friendship was a bit of a challenge, but once he understood I saw him as an independent member of my crew, his personality evolved swiftly. He convinced Probie to learn English so she could interact with us."

"And has she done so?"

"We're getting there. Ship and Probie can exchange information at an astounding rate. What would take me weeks or more to do with a new race of people, Ship has been able to do in a matter of minutes."

"And that was?"

"He shared our history, language, and his personal experiences since first meeting us. She shared her history, location of origin, and more. They've developed a bond of sorts. She has asked me what is to be done with her now that we have captured her."

"And that brings us to the next part of the discussion," replied Jeannie. "Suggestions, opinions, options?"

"Why not ask her to sign on with us? She'd make a fine scout if she would work with EX2," suggested Amanda.

"Personally, I'd like to have a look at her tech," grinned Moira Duncan. "See if she has any tricks we could add to the mix for us all."

"The other options are to destroy it or turn it loose," sighed Sheila Singh.

"Agreed," sighed Jeannie. "I don't like either of those options, but, since we're agreed that Probie is a sentient being, we need to handle this as we would any other alien life form we might encounter. Linsey, go back and have a chat with her, see if she has any ideas about what she'd like to do."

"On it, Admiral," smiled Linsey as she rose and fled the briefing room.

"Jeannie, you're not going to put that probe in the passenger area and make it my problem, are you?" grinned Miriam Holbrooke.

"Don't tempt me," chuckled Jeannie. "No, actually, I like the idea of having the probe work for us as an advance scout. With her stealth abilities she could hit a system, then let us know if it is safe to explore."

"Aye, there's a possible problem with that, Admiral."

"Talk to me, Moira."

"Well, that probe isn't very large, and it has made no attempt to return home, although it seems to know the right direction. I suspect it doesn't have interstellar capabilities. If it doesn't, it would have to ride along in the cargo hold of a ship to reach another system."

"Hmm, that does present a problem," mused Jeannie.

"Not if that ship is the Orca," said Sheila. "Orca could stop near a system, launch the probe, then stay dark until we got the all-clear. If it was a *no* then we could scoop up the probe and retreat."

"Forgive me, Captain Singh," said Morthel, "but Orca's task is to protect Reacher. EX2 is the explorer. However, I do like the idea of staying back, shielded, and letting the elusive probe take the first look at the situation."

"Captain Morthel has a point," said Amanda, "but right now this is all speculation. First we have to convince Probie to join the fleet."

"She has asked to do just that," said Linsey, as she returned. "Actually, she asked to remain close to Friendship. Ship explained about the fleet and how Admiral Sorenson is in command. She fully understands, and has requested to join the fleet since, like the rest of us, she has no way to get home."

"All right, Linsey, as the Officer in charge of Alien Relations, what do you recommend?"

"Admiral, I recommend we accept Probie into the fleet. She understands what her role will be and has asked to join us to perform that task. She is an AI, Admiral, intelligent, but created to perform a task. This will ensure her greater safety yet allow her to perform her original function.

"If we accept her, she will allow Ship to make a few subtle adjustments to her programming so she can interact with the rest of us organics."

"Organics?"

"Her words."

Jeannie chuckled at that, glanced around the table then returned her attention to Linsey. "All right, Linsey, go back and welcome the newest member of our fleet. Let me know as soon as she can interact with Organics, I want to speak with her personally. Oh, and ask her if she has interstellar capabilities."

"On my way, Admiral," smiled Linsey, as she stood and hurried out of the room.

A few minutes later Linsey was back on the comms. "da Silva to Admiral Sorenson."

"Here, Linsey. What's the good word?"

"The newest member of the fleet does have interstellar capabilities, but just enough to make single system jumps. There was no way for her to return to her original home. She says she will look forward to your visit."

"Thank you, Linsey. Well done. Come back to us now. Sorenson out.

"Well, there you go, we not only have our own war ship now, but our own independent intelligent probe. Our chances for long range survival just went way up.

"Now we come to it. We've been in this system well over two years. Are we finished here? Is there more to learn, salvage, other?"

"I think we're about finished, Jeannie," said Moira. "We've got Orca all ready, the Reacher and smaller ships all have the new upgrades, and our supply of metals is in good shape."

Jeannie grinned at her. "What's this I hear about you and Dorind taking over half Sheila's fighter bay for a cache of metals?"

"Aye, well, you can never have too many spare parts, can you, and there was more than enough room."

"How much metal do you have there, Moira?"

"Enough to build a dozen more fighter ships for Orca, you know, in case we might need them one day."

"Better to have the weapon and not need it than to need it and not have it?"

"Aye, Jeannie, that was the reasoning."

"I like it, Moira. So, we're done here?"

"I believe so."

"Captains? Anybody got any reasons to stick around longer?"

Nobody spoke for a moment, then Miriam chuckled. "If we stay any longer, Admiral, my people will start calling it a space colony."

"If we don't go exploring soon, Admiral, my crew will be looking for other jobs. Lilly already spends more time on Orca than she does here," grinned Morthel.

"All right, Mandy, take F1, plus Morthel, Linsey, Sessas, and Probie with you, head out to the Morar system. Take Captain Grill with you as well so he can meet Ka'Ron and start that negotiation. The rest of us will stay here and break down our operations, store whatever we want to take with us, then we'll join you there as soon as we can.

"That's it, people, start gathering up the toys, we're heading out. I'll go down for a chat with Probie while Amanda gathers her small fleet."

Chapter #15

Civil War

While Amanda packed up for a trip and gathered what she'd need, called for Captain Grill, and filled him in, Jeannie went to the cargo bay. "Greetings, Five," said Thirteen. "I was just chatting with our new friend here."

"Oh?"

"Yes, Probie has a good mind, Five."

"As do you, SUVI 13," said a soft feminine voice. "I greet you, SUVI 5, Admiral Sorenson of the fleet. This one is ready to serve."

"I greet you, Probie, and welcome you to the fleet."

"Thank you, Admiral. Do you have a task for this one?"

"I do. I'm sending four ships to the next system. I want you to go with them, and, as they near the system I want you to go on ahead and discover if there are any other ships in the area besides ours. If there are, relay that information to Vice-Admiral Drake aboard F1."

"Understood, Admiral. This one has not yet met Vice-Admiral Drake, but SUVI 13 holds her in high esteem. She is to command the mission?"

"She is."

"Understood."

"Ah, here she comes now. Mandy, my love, this is our newest addition to the fleet. Her name is Probie and she will accompany you on this mission."

"Welcome to the fleet, Probie. I'm looking forward to working with you."

"This one is ready for service, Vice-Admiral. Orders?"

"Once we launch, stay close to Friendship until we near the Morar system, then scout ahead to make certain we'll be the only ships in the air there, or to warn us of impending danger."

"Understood, Vice-Admiral."

"So, is everybody aboard and ready?"

"Ship prepped and ready, ma'am," grinned SUVI 9.

"Morthel, Linsey, Sessas, you guys ready?"

"Ready, Vice-Admiral."

"And we're off," grinned Amanda, as she turned back to Jeannie and hugged her tightly. "See you in a couple of weeks."

"Be careful, Mandy. I'll get there as quick as I can."

Amanda stepped aboard the ship and the hatch closed behind her. Jeannie stepped well back as the big bay doors began to open. A few minutes later the four ships and probe slipped out into space and shot away.

Jeannie was on her way back to her office when she met Rhonda coming the other way. "Come on, Admiral, let's head down to Simple Pleasures and take your mind off your troubles."

"My mind off my troubles? You mean sit there watching you drool over that blue-eyed girl who serves there?"

"Hey, I'll have you know I don't drool," chuckled Rhonda, "but I will admit seeing her is one of the top three reasons for suggesting we go there."

"Oh yeah? What are the other two?"

"I want to take your mind off your troubles for a little while, and I want to see if Alli has baked another of those cakes like Jake baked a few weeks ago. Dang that was tasty."

"And so was the girl?"

"Dammit, Jeannie," sputtered Rhonda, as her cheeks reddened, and Jeannie laughed. "Fine, okay, yes, the girl tastes even better than she looks. Happy now?"

"Yes I am," chuckled Jeannie, "and thank you for cheering me up."

"All part of the service," grinned Rhonda. "Let's go." Smiling, they headed off to Simple Pleasures together.

* * * * *

As the four ships and probe slipped out into space the voice of F1 spoke. "It is a pleasure to serve you again, Vice-Admiral Drake. To the Orca?"

"To the Morar system, F1, Planet Tarion is our destination."

"Course laid in and ship is ready to sail, Vice-Admiral."

"Hit it, Six."

"Vice-Admiral, may I ask, are we expecting battle?"

"No, F1, this is a diplomatic mission. Yes, the admiral sent me in her personal fighter ship. I imagine she believes I'll be a lot safer in a fighter ship with a crew of savage SUVI to protect me." That brought a round of chuckles from the crew.

"Then we'll all strive to meet those expectations," said the voice of the ship.

"Ship, we've flown together many times, and I have the utmost confidence in your abilities. It's a pleasure to sail with you again. Nine, what's our estimated arrival time?"

"We should arrive in three days, Vice-Admiral."

"Okay, Nine, choose a partner and get some rest. I get the day shift and you get nights."

That made him laugh. "Okay, Seven, you and I are on nights. Get some sleep."

Two and a half days later they were nearing the system. Amanda called for half speed while Probie shot on ahead. Three hours later she received the first message from the probe. "No ships, satellites, or other artificial craft detected. One message intercepted. Transmitting now.

"This message is for the Wandering Fleet. By the time you receive this I could be dead. We are engulfed in a civil war, and the old ship will soon be overrun. I wish you well, Admiral, and regret I will not get to fly with you again. Say goodbye to Sessas for me. Ka'Ron out."

"Sessas, Morthel, Linsey, did you get that?"

"We did," replied all three Captains.

"Let's get in there and see what's going on." With that F1 blasted away with EX2, Friendship, and Retriever close behind. An hour and a half put them in orbit above the planet. Their sensors showed them the situation below. The old ship Ka'Ron was trying to refit was surrounded by thousands of warriors, steadily pushing back the defenders.

"All right, Morthel, Linsey, Sessas, options, opinions."

It was Sessas who replied instantly. "Ka'Ron friend. Set down ships, shields up, protect Ka'Ron ship, his people."

"Morthel, Linsey?"

"What she said," replied Linsey.

"I like it, Vice-Admiral," agreed Morthel.

"Make it happen, people. Nine, get us down there, full shields."

"Full shields, aye. Going down."

Everyone on the ground stopped fighting to watch as the four ships dropped swiftly towards the ground, spreading out to surround the old ship. With the new ships on the ground, their shields raised, it was impossible for the aggressors to get past the barrier to engage the enemy. The war was effectively brought to a halt.

"Ka'Ron to Admiral Sorenson."

"Jeannie's not here, Ka'Ron. This is Amanda. Want to come aboard and tell me what's going on?"

"It will be a pleasure, Captain Drake. May I bring a guest or two with me?"

"Absolutely. Stand still now."

They appeared in F1 in a flash of light to be greeted by Amanda. "Nine, bring Morthel, Captain Grill, Sessas, and SUVI 20 aboard as well, would you please?"

"Aye, Vice-Admiral."

"Vice-Admiral?" asked Ka'Ron, as he gently embraced Sessas who had just stepped through the transporter.

"Yes. I got a promotion, Ka'Ron. Ah, everybody's here." She introduced them then settled everyone is the small seats. "All right now, Ka'Ron, tell us what happened here?"

"As you know, the last time your fleet was here, one of our people tried to capture the admiral. That man is the chieftain of the largest clan. He convinced his fellow chieftain that we were defiling the sacred ship and they rose up against us.

"This woman is Wel'Lyn, Chieftain of the Me'Ten Clan, the smallest clan, but the traditional protectors of the sacred ship. She has defended us as best she can, but we are horribly outnumbered. It's only a matter of time before we are overrun."

The old priest rose painfully, leaning on his staff for balance. "Will you help us, friend of Ka'Ron?"

"Let's talk about that," replied Amanda. "This man is Captain Grill. His ship was also hurled into this sector, as was our own. However, Captain Grill wasn't as lucky as we were, and his ship is beyond repair.

"We brought Captain Grill with us because he has a small crew of experienced spacefarers, but no ship, and no way to get home. We hoped you could take him and his crew in, let them help you get your ship back into space, go exploring once again."

Ka'Ron and his companions were eyeing up Captain Grill. He rose and spoke softly. "I and my people are not warriors, we're explorers. We've been brought to this area of space with no way to get home. We're lost, and imagined dead by those we left behind on the home world. We have no way to survive, and no purpose or reason to exist.

"Admiral Sorenson suggested that, with your assistance, we could continue to explore the universe, and that we in turn, could help you fly your ship. This would allow you to escape your enemies without further bloodshed. We have three engineers, and a few bridge officers as well as two dozen more experienced crew to offer."

"You would help us return the sacred ship to the stars? Help my clan learn the ways of life in the sky?" asked Wel'lyn.

"Yes, that's why I've come. Please, good people, we can help each other."

"Ancient Ka'Ron, this is a way for us to survive and get the sacred ship back to the stars as you wanted."

"This is acceptable to you, Wel'lyn?"

"It is."

"Elder?"

"This is the answer we prayed for, Ancient One. Accept this man and his people."

"Agreed, then," said Ka'Ron, as he rose and extended his hand to Captain Grill, who shook it. "Come, we should return to the ship so you can see what we're up against for repairs. Vice-Admiral Drake, do you think the admiral will allow your people to help us?"

"I do, Ka'Ron. I'll send messages to her right now letting her know what's happening here. She'll arrive soon, I'm sure. You take Captain Grill back to your ship and I'll see what I can do to settle the hostilities down here a bit."

Once Ka'Ron and his companion transported away, Amanda turned to SUVI 9. "What's going on out there, Nine?"

"They've discovered the shields and are trying to break through them."

"Any chance of that happening?"

"Not in this lifetime."

"Alright then, is there any way we can send a repulson burst through the shields without killing them?"

"Not really, ma'am."

"Okay, okay, Thirteen would tell me to use my brain," she sighed. The SUVI all chuckled at that. "All right, let's try this. Go back to your ships, watch the sensors for anyone who looks like a leader, then transport them a few kilometers away. Sooner or later they should get the idea that they're out gunned here."

The others were grinning as they transported back to their own ships. "Six, can we contact Probie from here?"

"Easily. F1 calling Probie."

"Probie is here. Awaiting orders, Vice-Admiral Drake."

"Probie, I need you to take this message back to the admiral, aboard Reacher. Jeannie, we're under siege here, but unharmed. We arrived in the middle of a civil war but have managed to enforce a temporary break in the hostilities. Ka'Ron and Captain Grill seem to be getting along well. Miss you. Amanda."

"Message received, Vice-Admiral. Returning to Reacher."

"Probie just went super-light, Vice-Admiral. It'll take her three days to get there at best speed."

"And another three or more for Jeannie to get back here. Might as well settle in, guys. We've got a few days to kill. Seven, is the transport thing working?"

"I've transported a few of them far away, but it's not slowing them down. Looks like Sessas is transporting a dozen at a time, dropping them in a swamp."

"Love the way she thinks," grinned Amanda. "Follow her lead."

* * * * *

By the end of the second day it looked bad to Amanda, she was afraid they'd burn out the transporters, but suddenly the attackers withdrew a short distance. Apparently, they too needed rest. Plopping back into her seat, Amanda reached for her comms. "Drake to Ka'Ron."

"Ka'Ron here, Vice Admiral."

"How's it going over there?"

"The engineers from your ships are making a tremendous difference. I'm told we can fabricate the few remaining parts needed from Reacher's store of metals, if the admiral approves."

"I'm sure she will. Are you capable of flight yet?"

"Negative, Vice-Admiral. We need a couple of new parts, and the rest of Captain Grill's crew before we reach for the stars."

"Understood, Ka'Ron. Drake out." She sighed then turned to her crew. "What do you think, Nine, is Probie close enough to transmit yet?"

"Doubtful, Vice-Admiral."

"Hmm. I wonder. Drake to Sessas."

"Sessas here."

"Sessas, your ship is carrying heavier weapons than the rest of us. Do you have anything that will make a big show, something sustained?"

"Twenty here, Vice-Admiral. What do you have in mind?"

"Ideally, I'd like you to fly a tight circle around us, just outside the shields, lay down a path of destruction to demonstrate the folly of making a sudden rush at us."

"Sessas understand, can do. Tentee, on guns. We go, Vice-Admiral."

Amanda grinned as she watched the sensors. Retriever rose into the air, then faced the enemy and opened fire. She flew a slow enclosing circle around the ships then returned to her station and settled to the ground again. Damn, those two made an efficient team.

There was now a ten-foot-wide trench all the way around the ships. Those watching shuddered as SUVI 20's sharp shooting blasted apart trees, boulders, and more, while the big energy cannon melted the soil and debris into a molten mass. The message had been delivered.

"Drake to Sessas."

"Here."

"Well done, Captain Sessas. Tell Twenty I'm glad she wasn't shooting at me."

"Will tell," came Sessas' hissing laugh.

"Think that got the message across, Nine?"

"It was truly impressive. Not a single soul was harmed, but it was made clear to them that none could survive direct conflict. I'd say it was effective."

"Let's hope so, because I doubt the transporters could take much more. Drake to Captain Morthel."

"Morthel here."

"Morthel, is Theo Billings still your engineer or did you lose him to Orca?"

"Theo is still on my crew, Vice-Admiral. Right now he's aboard Ka'Ron's ship. Do you need repairs?"

"Negative, Morthel. I was just looking for a more detailed progress report."

"I'll contact him, tell him you need adjustments to your transporter."

"Morthel, you're the best. Drake out."

A few moments later a young man appeared on the transporter pad. "You've got a problem, Vice-Admiral?"

"No, Theo, I just wanted an honest opinion of Ka'Ron's ship. Can it ever really fly or are we feeding a dream for him."

"No, she'll fly easy enough. She was a tough ship, still in good shape for the most part. The hull is intact, most of the interior survived the crash, in fact, I think they actually made a good landing and broke off a landing strut, that's why she's on such a hard lean, but most everything else inside works."

"Then what's the problem? I'd like to get her up to orbit so we can make repairs in peace."

"Not enough crew, that's the problem, that and the engines haven't fired in centuries. The weapons look good, though. They'll need help getting the food processors active again, but they managed to lay in plenty of supplies before it all went to hell on them."

"If they have functional weapons, why didn't they use them to defend themselves?" asked SUVI 6.

"Couldn't tell you for sure," sighed Ensign Billings. "I did ask, but Ka'Ron said it wasn't honorable to use modern weapons on an enemy who only had a spear."

"Sounds like a poor survival strategy to me," grinned Six.

"Second that," chuckled Theo. "You come at me with a spear, and I'll use a blaster on you. However, that's not how they work, I guess. The admiral might want to be aware of that, you know, for future reference."

"And she will be, Theo," said Amanda. "Count on it. So, we only need a crew and a few spare parts?"

"Ah-huh. I can fabricate the parts on Reacher in a couple of hours. The Maccay will be enough crew to get her flying, and they can give the rest of the Morar on-the-job training."

"What kind of parts do you need? Could we rob a few from our ships to get her to orbit?"

"Nope, sorry, our igniters aren't compatible with their engines. We've got the old ones to use as a guide for making new ones, but we need the equipment on the Reacher or Orca for that."

"Hmm, you know, I think the fleet needs at least one more small ship."

"Oh?"

"Yes, we have an explorer, a rescue ship, a couple of fighters, two salvage ships, a diplomat ship, but we should have a mobile repair ship, don't you think?"

"You mean, so that if something happens, like it did on Stormy, temporary repairs could be made on the ground instead of waiting for the big ships to arrive, or for the salvage ships to tow us back."

"That's what I'm thinking ... What the hell is going on now?" A loud voice was suddenly heard from outside.

"Attention, demons from the stars. Return the sacred ship to us and leave. If you do not we will kill you all."

"What??? Is he serious?"

"You have until the sun is at its highest to decide your fate."

"Apparently he is," chuckled Six.

"On screen."

"On screen, Aye." Outside their ship stood a man wearing a brightly colored headdress. He was flanked by several others. "Six, transport that fool in here."

"Transporting now."

The man appeared in a flash of light. He tried to raise his spear, but SUVI 7 threw him against the bulkhead and disarmed him, then shoved him into a seat. Amanda stepped close and glared down at him. He tried to leap at her but was easily held down by Seven.

Amanda waited until he was still, resigned to his fate. "Are you stupid? Can you think, reason, understand simple things?" The translator on her uniform spoke her words in Ka'Ron's voice.

"I should kill you for speaking to me that way."

"Answer my question, can you understand simple things?"

"Yes," he snarled.

"Have you ever fallen and hurt yourself?"

"What? Yes, as a child."

"How far did you fall?"

"What?"

"How far did you fall?"

"From a tree, twice the height of a man."

"Do you understand what would happen if you fell from the top of that sacred ship of yours?"

"No man could survive such a fall."

"No, you couldn't. If you try to attack us, I'll take you up to twice the height of that ship, then drop you."

"You can't ..."

"Yes I can, the same way I brought you here. Six, send him back, but drop him from about twelve feet up."

"Dropping the enemy, aye," grinned SUVI 6, as he worked the control panel.

Outside there was a scream of terror as the man found himself suddenly high above his confused companions. He flailed his arms and legs as he plummeted to the ground to be helped up by the others. There was a lot of garbled conversation then he leaned heavily on another and limped away.

"Think he got the message, Vice-Admiral?"

"I do, Theo. Curious?"

He laughed at that. "You know me too well."

"That guy is typical of bad leadership, my friend. For him it's all about what he wants, to hell with the cost to his followers. By doing what I did, I made it personal. He now knows what will happen to him if he sends his people at us. We'll let the shields deal with them, but we'll grab him and drop him from a high place, and he knows full well we can do it."

"So, he's willing to sacrifice his people, but not himself. That was good thinking."

"Yeah, Thirteen's teachings sunk in, I guess. Don't tell him."

"Not a word," chuckled Theo.

* * * * *

Jeannie had called a meeting with the captains and senior officers as well as the passenger representatives. "Are we all here? Excellent, tell me good things, people. Are we ready to go?"

"Orca is ready to sail, Admiral."

"Reacher is ready, Admiral. We've got the small ships aboard and everything's ready. Just give the command."

"Miriam, do the passengers have any reason to linger here?"

"None, Admiral. We're ready if you are."

"All right then, ..."

"Bridge to Admiral Sorenson. We're receiving messages from Probie. The Morar planet is embroiled in a civil war. Our advance ships are requesting immediate assistance."

"Understood, bridge. Captains, get this fleet to the Morar system, all possible speed."

"Aye, Admiral," said Sheila, as she and her staff leapt to their feet, Sheila grabbing for her comm. "Orca, this is the captain, six to transport. Bring us home and warm up the engines." They disappeared in a flash of light.

Rhonda looked to Jake. "Tell me we're battened down."

"Ship is ready to sail at your command, Captain."

"Rhonda to the bridge."

"Bridge here."

"Anita, aim us at the Morar system and hit it, all possible speed. Don't wait for me." The Reacher was already gone from the salvage system before she reached the bridge.

* * * * *

For five days the army remained, did a lot of posturing, but didn't attack. On the sixth day the rest of the fleet arrived. At the sight of Orca slowly settling to the ground, the army fled.

Suddenly, Jeannie appeared in the transport area of F1 to catch Amanda in her arms. "By all the gods, Mandy, I miss you when you're not there."

"I miss you too, my super SUVI. Come sit, and I'll give you a full report." She took Jeannie by the hand and led her to the seating area. "Okay, we arrived to find Ka'Ron and friends under attack by the guy who tried to capture you. We scared them back then landed and locked our shields around his ship to hold them at bay.

"We were transporting bunches of them away and dropping them in a swamp, but that didn't deter them enough. Next Sessas flew a circle around us with guns blazing, making a trench, and demonstrating the stupidity of continuing the attack. They postured a lot, but there was no loss of life."

"Excellent, Mandy, now tell me the part you're not telling me."

Amanda sighed. "How do you always do that?"

"SUVI secret, now talk."

"Okay, well the king or chief or whatever he is just wouldn't learn, so I transported him here, told him to back off or I'd take him up above the big ship and drop him on his head. When we sent him back, we dropped him from a few meters up so he'd get the idea. That seemed to work."

"I love it, Mandy. How's the work on Ka'Ron's ship going?"

"According to Theo, they just need to fabricate a few parts, then they're ready to go."

"Good to know. Once we've got her into orbit, the repairs can be finished, Linsey and Lilly can top up our supplies, and we'll be ready to go exploring."

"Can we top up here? I don't think the natives are going to be willing to trade with us anymore."

"I'm not asking their permission, nor offering trade. They gave up that right when they attacked you. We'll take what we need then leave them to their fate."

Amanda just nodded. This new warrior SUVI was a bit harder and less compassionate than before, but this was what she'd ask Jeannie to do, and she could see Jeannie's focus was still on doing the best for her combined people.

A few hours later there were cheers aboard the fleet, and howls of frustration and protest from the ground, as the Kreenon rose slowly from the ground where she's landed so many centuries before. The Morar were returning to the stars.

In the end, they actually took very little from the planet, mostly more plant samples so Lilly Peters could help her father bring the hydroponics bay of the Orca up to speed. Retriever, EX4, and F1 flew with EX2 as guards while Lilly collected her samples, but there was no attempt to interfere.

* * * * *

Ten days later, Suvi-jean called a meeting of the captains and senior staff. They met in the briefing room of the Reacher. "All requested personnel present, Admiral Sorenson."

"Thank you, Vice-Admiral Drake. Ka'Ron, I see that both you and Captain Grill are here. Which of you is to command the Kreenon?"

"Captain Grill will be in command, Admiral," he replied.

Grill chuckled. "Actually, Admiral, my new friend, Ka'Ron, has never commanded a ship so he has asked me to take on that task while he assumes the post of First Officer. However, the Kreenon is a Morar ship, so as soon as Ka'Ron feels comfortable with command we will exchange roles and I will become the First Officer."

"I like it," smiled Jeannie. "Alright then, until you sort yourselves out, I want both of you to attend the captains' meetings. Now, gentlemen, report. Is your ship ready to sail?"

"Engineer Duncan has fully inspected the Kreenon and declared her fit for service, Admiral," replied Grill. "We now officially request permission to join your fleet."

"Grill, you do understand we could one day be forced into conflict. You will also be under my direct command."

"I do, Admiral. We have agreed that, in such circumstances, the Morar would take full control of the ship and the Maccay would retire to quarters. In this way the Kreenon could defend herself, yet the Maccay would be able to retain their vow of non-violence."

"I was the weapons officer on my ship when we encountered the Wrax, Admiral," said Ka'Ron. "I've trained several of my kin folk to operate the weapons systems."

"So your ship is ready to sail?"

"It is, Admiral."

"Excellent. Permission to join the fleet granted. Captain Singh, is the Orca ready to sail?"

"Ready and awaiting your order, Admiral," was the smiling reply.

"Captain Moore?"

"All small ships aboard, and Reacher is ready to sail on your command, Admiral."

"Excellent. People, we've been hanging around here for over two years now. Probie reports the next system has a lot of space junk circling one planet in the Goldilocks Zone, but nothing moving under its own power. I think it's time we went exploring again. Return to your ships, captains, we set sail in one hour."

The meeting broke up and everyone hurried away to prepare for travel. Back in the café, Maxi got a cryptic message. "One hour." A bright smile lit up her face and she grabbed Alli by the arm, then whispered in her ear. Alli tossed aside her apron and fled the café.

Kar was briefing a team of security officers when Alli poked her head into the office and waved her arm. Kar grinned and set aside her tablet. "Dismissed, people. We're about to set sail." She hurried out, where Alli grabbed her hand and together they set out for the observation room. They arrived with bare minutes to spare. A moment later the comms pinged.

"Kar, is that you in the observation cone?"

"Busted."

"Your captain had better be able to get her dessert once the ship is underway."

"The captain's companion has things completely under control," replied Kar. "Your dessert will be ready and waiting for you."

"Then all's well in my world. Enjoy the show, we're counting down. Moore out."

Jeannie and Amanda were on the bridge with Rhonda. "Kar and Alli sneaked off to the observation cone for the take off?" asked Amanda.

"Yes, they seem to like that spot. All yours, Admiral."

"Thank you, Captain Moore. Comms, fleet wide."

"Fleet wide, aye. Go ahead, Admiral."

"Attention all captains. Your course has been transmitted, are you ready to sail?"

"Course laid in; Orca ready to sail."

"Course laid in, Kreenon ready to sail, Admiral."

"On my mark, three, two, one, engage star drive."

Those people on the ground looking up saw three bright pinpoints of light suddenly wink out as the Reacher and her sister ships leapt through space toward an uncertain destiny as the last remains of several species continued to fight for survival in an uncaring universe.

Aboard the flagship Reacher, in the forward observation room, Alli got another kiss where the entire galaxy could see.

The End

And now for a peek at the next adventure in the Forgotten Worlds series:

UNITE

by

Prudence MacLeod

A Curse From the Past

"You are certain none remain?"

"None, sir. The entire system has been cleansed of all resistance. A few scattered bands of fugitives are all that's left."

"Then set out the auto defenses, full perimeter. No one, no species must ever discover what evil was wrought here. The knowledge they possessed must perish with them."

"Yes, sir, destructors deployed, observation posts manned. If any species comes here, they will never leave."

"Very good. Set course for home."

Grounded

"Approaching the next star system, Admiral. Eighteen planets, four in the Zone. Probie reports plenty of space junk, all ancient, nothing under power."

Suvi-jean Sorenson, admiral of the small fleet of ships holding the last humans alive in the galaxy, nodded and turned to the small alien woman across the table. "Looks like you're clear to go, Captain Morthel."

Smiling brightly, she rose to her feet and snapped off a salute. "Thank you, Admiral. I'll prepare my ship." Jeannie smiled as she watched the Earalithian woman hurry away.

In ancient times, the Earalith ruled a vast empire containing thousands of star systems. Morthel was one of only eleven Earalith still alive. No longer a shy, introverted minor princess of a royal family, she was now the energetic captain of the fleet's main explorer ship, EX2.

Morthel arrived at her ship, Explorer Two, EX2 as they called her, to hear the sounds of a crying baby. "Crew all aboard?"

"Crew is aboard, Captain," replied SUVI 13, the ship's main surface explorer and bodyguard. All SUVI (survivor of unknown viral infection) have enhanced abilities and use the number of their survival instead of a name. This man was the thirteenth survivor.

"Lock her down. Three, request launch."

"Ship is locked down."

"We have launch clearance."

"Take us out, Three. Aim for the nearest planet in the Goldilocks Zone, then hit it."

"Aye, Captain, launching. Target acquired; ship is underway."

"Thank you, Three." The baby was still crying, so Morthel turned to her security officer, Connie Kim. "Want a break?"

"Thank you, Captain. I have no idea why she's fussing."

"I do," said Morthel, as she accepted the child from her mother's arms. Earalith have two thumbs on each hand, and little SUVI 21 loved it when she got to wrestle with Morthel's thumbs. Morthel held the baby in one arm and wiggled her thumbs, which were immediately grabbed in tiny fists. The child stopped fussing and giggled. Since the birth of Twenty-One had proved the SUVI can reproduce, bearing children with SUVI abilities, the SUVI had been confirmed in official records as a species in their own right.

"You just want to hear the captain make funny sounds, so she'll be embarrassed in front of the crew, don't you?" cooed Morthel, as she played with the child in her arms. "You're just trying to make me lose all respect and my reputation as a fierce captain." The child was laughing now and wrestling with those agile thumbs.

"Approaching planet One, Captain."

"Thank you, Three." Morthel's next sentence was lost in the frightened wail of the baby in her arms. Her eyes snapped back to the child for only a heartbeat. "Dammit. Shields!"

The shields went up just as the first salvo hit the ship. Further fire was erratic and scattered as a shielded ship is nearly impossible to target. "Get us on the ground! Find a spot where we can inspect for damage."

As the agile ship dropped toward the planet, her captain turned back to the child in her arms. She was quiet once again. "So, you're another intuitive, like Eighteen and Twenty, are you? Good to know."

"Captain?"

Morthel turned to Connie and Thirteen, the baby's parents. "Twenty-One is SUVI, as we know, and I believe she's fully intuitive. She was fussing because she sensed danger. I was able to distract her for a while, but her sudden cry of alarm clued me in. She's quiet now, so I'm guessing the immediate danger is past." She rose and handed the baby back to its mother.

"Where are we, Three?"

"Flying over ruins, Captain. There's an open spot up ahead, could have been a space port at one time. Possibly a good place to check for damage."

"Sensors, anything moving?"

"Just us, Captain, and no other life signs."

"All right, Three, set her down. How's the atmosphere?"

"Looks breathable, Captain."

"Good to know. Commander Peters."

"Captain?"

"Care to babysit our youngest crewman while the rest of us check for damages?"

Lilly Peters, the ship's botanist, chuckled at that. "Sure, why not? There's nothing growing around here anyway. "Come to Aunt Lilly, Twenty-One. We'll hang out on the ship while Mom and Dad keep the engineers from being eaten by giant predators."

"Not funny, Lilly," grumbled Thirteen. "I've still got scars from planet Stormy and those damned predators." He swept the huge scatter blaster to the ready position and Connie opened the hatch. He leaped through with Connie right behind him. "Anything?"

"I've got nothing."

"Me neither. Looks clear, Captain." At his call, Morthel led her pilot and engineer out of the ship. They were followed by the six maintenance personnel assigned to the botanist.

After a thorough inspection of the hull, followed by full diagnostics of all systems, EX2 was given a clean bill of health. "Looks like we're good, Captain," said the engineer. "EX2 is tough all right. We took one direct hit, but the shields kept the rest from making contact."

Morthel noticed the man never took his eyes off the hull of the ship and seemed nervous. "Thank you, Brodie. All right, people, everybody back aboard. Thirteen, speculate, what happened?"

"Looks like this place is another dead planet, Captain Morthel. Offhand, I'd say they were at odds with somebody from somewhere else. I think we triggered another ancient planetary defense system. Whatever it was, it didn't try to follow us down."

"Our shields worked well," said Connie. "Maybe whatever it was is still up there looking for us."

"And maybe it turned away expecting something else down here to take over," sighed the engineer, Brodie Cortez. "There's no way to know for sure right now." He was still looking down at the ship's deck.

"So, do we return to the fleet, Captain?"

"Not yet. We're here to explore the planet, so we'll continue that mission. Lilly, see if you can raise the Reacher for me."

"Aye, Captain. EX2 calling Reacher, come in Reacher. EX2 calling Reacher, please respond."

"Reacher here, EX2. Rerouting you to Admiral Sorenson." A moment later Jeannie's voice reached them. "Sorenson here. What's up, Morthel?"

"We were hit by some sort of planetary defense system, Admiral. We're on the ground, but unharmed, the shields worked well."

"Do you need assistance?"

"Not at this time, but perhaps we've awakened something that could become a problem if there are more in the area."

"Understood. I'll ask Sessas to look into it. Sorenson out."

"Three, take us up and begin a standard grid search pattern. Brodie, keep those shields up just in case."

"Aye, Captain, shields are raised. Captain, do you believe it's safe to proceed?"

"I do. As you can see, our early warning system is sleeping peacefully." She was smiling at the baby in Connie Kim's arms.

Two hours later they found it, a vast city that spanned half a continent. Much of it had given way to the vegetation that was reasserting itself over the planet.

"Lilly, you on sensors?"

"I am, Captain. I've got plenty of life signs, but not seeing anything that looks truly organized. I'd say that the people who built this city are long gone, and the natural world is taking over."

"Any signs of automated defenses?"

"Sensors show no active power sources. SUVI sensors are quiet, no immediate threats indicated."

"Good to know," chuckled Morthel. "All stop."

"Ship is stopped, Captain."

"Thank you, Three."

"Captain?"

"Huh? Oh, sorry, Thirteen. Just thinking, that city is massive, easily equal to an Earalith capitol. That tells me there was a lot of tech at work down there at one time, and that would require vast amounts of energy. Lilly, poke around a bit, see if you can see anything that might suggest a generation plant."

"What's on your mind, Captain?"

"Thirteen, my friend, anything that could generate enough energy to run a city of that size would surely be of interest to main engineering."

"It would at that."

"Actually, I'd rather look for something else," said Lilly.

"Lilly?"

"Captain, enough people to fill that city would need a food supply second to none. I wonder, might there be a few remnants of that miracle for us to find."

"Getting ahead of myself again, was I?" chuckled Morthel. "Continue grid pattern, Three."

"Continuing grid search, aye." Morthel smiled as she felt the ship resume its forward motion.

* * * * *

At the end of shift Morthel ordered the ship into low orbit. "Anything on sensors, Lilly?"

"Nothing moving, Captain. Not on the ground, nor in space."

"Thirteen?"

Connie had to nudge him as she seemed lost in thought. "Huh?"

"The captain?"

"Oh, sorry Captain. No, nothing on SUVI sensors, neither mine nor the baby's."

Morthel sat beside him and spoke kindly. "What is it, Thirteen? What's eating at you?"

He sighed deeply and did not meet her eyes. "I didn't see it coming. That's my job, and I didn't see it coming."

"Nobody did," she replied. "Your special talent is possible futures, not sensing out hidden dangers."

"Maybe, but I should have. When we moved close to the first Earalith colony I sensed the danger, why not here?"

"It's worth noting," said SUVI 3, "that neither of the truly intuitives, Eighteen and Twenty, nor the admiral herself, sensed it either, or we'd have been forewarned. Don't beat yourself up over this one. We got down without a scratch, could have been worse."

"Yeah, I guess."

"So, take a look and see if we get out of here alive." That voice came from Ensign Brodie Cortez, an engineer on his first exploration trip. He had been so eager, Morthel had taken him on, but his tone caused her concern.

Thirteen's voice was cold and dangerous when he responded, sending a shiver through most of the small crew. "Was that an order?" As a former slave to Brodie's people in their underground colony, Thirteen didn't respond well to that tone.

Brodie shrank away and turned to the sensors. Morthel patted Thirteen's arm. "Easy, my friend, easy. Actually, that might not be a bad idea, but it can wait a few days, we've got a lot more to do before we start worrying about going home.

"Get some rest everyone. Three, Axel, Connie, and Twenty-One will take the first shift with me. Lilly, you and the rest get the second shift."

As Brodie headed for the sleeping quarters, Connie, baby in her arms, stepped in his path. "You're not in the Caverns now; best not to annoy a SUVI." She stepped away to the engineering station. "Shields at full, Captain."

Morthel looked up, saw Connie glance at Brodie's retreating back, then nodded. "Thank you, Officer Kim."

Thirteen stopped to kiss Connie and the baby goodnight. "Leave him to me," she whispered. "I'll handle it." He nodded and continued on to the sleeping booth. As a former slave, he'd had a strong reaction to the young man's tone of voice. He was a bit annoyed with himself for rising to the bait so easily.

The ship was on auto and those awake gathered near the pilot's station, talking softly to let the others sleep. "Three."

"Yes, Captain?"

"I have no idea at all of a slave's experience, but I do have plenty of experience on the other side of that coin. Have I ever used that tone with any of you?"

"You're the captain," chuckled Alec Hoff, crew chief of the maintenance people, "all captains sound like that."

"I'm serious, Alec. Three?"

"No, Morthel, you haven't."

Morthel looked thoughtful for a moment. "Antha would say we're two sides of a common coin, you and Thirteen from slavery and me from royalty. No matter the species, I'm sure there are similarities in the manner of interactions. Those times are long past for all of us. Three, if you ever hear me speak like that to any of the SUVI, any of the crew for that matter, tell me immediately."

"Captain?" Three grinned. "It would be unseemly for a pilot to chastise the captain."

Morthel chuckled at that. "Just say, 'Captain, flip a coin,' and I'll get the message. Yes, as captain I have to give orders, but there's a right way and a wrong way to do it. I watched Vice-Admiral Drake when she was captain, and I try very hard to follow her example."

"Captain, nobody on this crew has an issue with your style of command, or the fact you were promoted to captain. You're good and we all have full confidence in you."

"Thank you, Three."

Connie smiled. "Captain, you and Thirteen were friends before your promotion, and he's more than happy to see you in the role. Believe me, there are no issues here. He's just messed up a bit; he didn't sense the danger before it happened.

"No, ma'am, the problem here is Brodie. He was a baby when they landed on Elysium and spent all his life in the caverns working beside his father. He's a good engineer, but the open spaces are freaking him out. I doubt he's even looked outside the Reacher before coming aboard this ship. Hard not to look from EX2."

"Seriously?"

"Connie's right," said Alec. "I noticed him shaking when we left the ship to inspect for damage. I'll bet he had no idea this would happen and is totally freaked out by it."

"Thank you, Alec, I didn't notice that, and I should have."

"You can't catch everything, Captain. That's what you have us for," smiled Connie.

"All right, but let's keep an eye on him."

"We will, Captain, and I'll keep a reign on Thirteen as well."

"Good luck with that," chuckled Morthel.

Don't miss out!

Visit the website below and you can sign up to receive emails whenever Prudence MacLeod publishes a new book. There's no charge and no obligation.

https://books2read.com/r/B-A-ZKBBB-CSUQC

BOOKS 2 READ

Connecting independent readers to independent writers.

Also by Prudence MacLeod

Forgotten Worlds
Suvi
Echo of the Past
Survivors
Ship
Fleet

Watch for more at https://www.prudencemacleod.com/.

Telling a story is like knitting a sweater. Start with a ball of possibilities, pull out one small thread and begin. With luck and patience you will create something quite wonderful.

About the Author

On a far off windswept island Jennifer Crandall sits with her dogs and cats creating fantastic stories for all to enjoy. She publishes as JL Crandall, Prudence MacLeod, and Jenni Leigh.

Read more at https://www.prudencemacleod.com/.

www.ingramcontent.com/pod-product-compliance
Lightning Source LLC
Chambersburg PA
CBHW020943180626
46814CB00003B/914